eternal
REVENGE

LAQUITA CHERRY

http://laquitacherry.com

ISBN-13: 978-0-615-47756-5
ISBN-10: 0-615-47756-9

Jacket Design © www.laquitacherry.com
First Printing July 2018
Manufactured and Printed in the United Stated

ACKNOWLEDGEMENTS

First and foremost, I would love to thank The Most High. Thank you for blessing with a creative mind and the gift of writing. This book wouldn't be possible without you.

I would like to thank my family and friends, you guys rock!

I would like to also thank Maxie Wilson, Kadeli "Foogie" Henderson, Brittney Johnson, Damarcus Johnson, Felisha & Mateen Davis, Dedra Morris, LaTonya Pough, William "Willie JP" Pough, Terriel Garvey, Shantrell Bryant, Christopher Campbell, Janice Bing, Derrick Dollar, Kettler A. Danielle H., Regina Medina, Kenneth "KG" Green, Rodney & Harriette Wilson, Gloria Hayward, Sherry Pressley, Shannon Hunter, Shirley & Leon Smith, Cynthia & Clifford Hunter, Sharon Wilson, Reggie Todd, April Tutson, Linda Tutson and Jacqueline Todd.

I dedicate this book to the entire beautiful city of Chicago! I dedicate this book to inspire the dreamers, hoping that this will give you that get up and go! I dedicate this book to the struggle. Believe in yourself and never give up. Stay positive and be encouraged!

-LaQuita

Malcom

Bright lights. Screaming crowds. Fans lined up around the block. That's the life I envision. My game is tight. My grades are good. My future is locked in place…almost.

Another guy in a three-piece suit follows me off the court and into the locker room. "Great game, Malcolm."

I knew how to play the part. My parents had warned me about the legion of coaches and big-name recruiters who would be making appearances as my senior year at Westinghouse.

My father, the long-time principal, darted out of nowhere, his hand extended, practically salivating at the prospect of gaining footing on a college campus by way of me – the good son. "Hello, there. I'm Dale Harris, the principal and this talented young man's father."

The recruiter flashed a smile at him, while keeping one eye on me. "Nice to meet you, sir. I wondered if I could have a minute with your son."

"You don't need his permission. I'll talk to you, but I only have a minute," I said, not to be rude, but the truth was, so many recruiters had come around, I had a hard time distinguishing one from the other. As long as I got a scholarship to a good school, I knew I was well on my way to a career in the NBA. That's all that mattered. It was my way out of this life.

The recruiter went through the same speech I'd heard dozens of others like him give. I did the obligatory nodding and smiling where appropriate. The truth was I hadn't made a decision yet. All I knew was that I was going places because of who I was and what I did. Despite what my father claimed, he didn't make me what I was. I made me.

I thanked the man for stopping by and went on my way, ignoring the scowl on my father's face. They followed me every time I made a move these days. My brother's life choices were my burden to carry as far as my father was concerned. I was supposed to be an example to him, even though he was older than me. I was supposed to be the antithesis of my drug-dealing, fast-living older brother. I'm the one my father hung all his failed hopes and dreams on, and I hated being put in that position. The pressure was too much for a kid. It was too much for anyone. How it ended up falling on my shoulders, I'll never know.

"I'm so proud of you, my baby boy," my mom, Delila, was the perfect woman as far as I was concerned. She deserved every good thing life had to offer, and if it was the last thing I did, I'd get it for her. Lord knows my father wasn't trying to do that. He did what he was supposed to do. I'm sure he had good intentions, but somewhere along the way

– maybe because my brother lost his way or because he'd forgotten that there are no true secrets in life. None.

I hugged her, as I often could. I couldn't help it. There was no one on earth I loved more than my Mama. She was everything. "I'm so proud of you." I leaned toward the stove. "What are you cooking? It smells good."

She blushed like I'd discovered a secret. "Your favorite." She smacked my hand. "Don't act like you don't know what that is. Everyone knows how much you love your flapjacks. They're piled a mile high on the counter. What happened? You're too tall to see anything shorter than six-feet-tall?"

"What is that smell? It's making my stomach growl." My father pulled out a chair at the kitchen table, threw this morning's sports page on the table, and said the same thing he says every morning, "Don't just stand there, Delila. Where's my coffee? I know you didn't forget. You never forget."

My parents had been married twenty-five years. Longer than most couples I knew. Lately though, the air between them had grown thick. They still talked and laughed and sometimes danced in the kitchen, but something – perhaps the glint in my mother's big brown eyes – had dimmed. Something had changed, ever so slightly, and I couldn't for the life of me, figure out what it was. All I knew is it was there, stuck somewhere between where he teased her about her "womanly duties" and where he more and more frequently forgot to answer her calls.

"Dale, you should know by now, I never forget anything. Never. Now, you can pick up that mess on the table and walk you behind over to the coffee pot that's been in the same exact spot for the last twenty-five years and pour yourself some." She winked at me. "Pour me one too while you're at it."

I tried not to laugh as I watched the expression on his face change from shock to humor and finally confusion. "Fine. I know where the coffee pot is. I know where everything in this house is. I ought to. I paid for all of it."

If my beautiful mother hadn't been standing there, I would have said something to him about being disrespectful to my mother, but with one look, she stopped me. I could see her struggle with how to respond.

"Watch yourself, Dale. You don't want to go there with me because I'll point out all the stuff I've done for you, for our boys, for your career, etc.

He must not have been in the mood to squabble with her because he walked over, gave her a gentle nudge, and planted a kiss on her cheek. "Can I call a truce, lovely lady?"

She gave him her infamous side eye, then giggled. "I don't know what I'm going to do with you. Sometimes, you're worse than the kids, you know that? I thought you were really trying to go there with me."

He scoffed at the idea. "Why would I do that? I may be a lot of things, but the last I checked, dumb wasn't one of them." He glanced at me. I hadn't stopped staring him directly in the eyes. "Did you tell your mother about the recruiter?"

I nodded. "Yes, sir."

She wrapped her arms around my waist. "Of course, he did. We don't keep secrets from each other. Not in this family."

I kissed the top of her head. "No, ma'am, we don't. Why don't you sit down? Let me serve you this morning."

She laughed as if I'd told her a joke. "You're going to serve me breakfast? The breakfast I made for you?" She teared up because she was laughing so hard. "Look at him. Trying to act like he's doing me a favor." She grabbed the platter of flapjacks and set them on the table in front of my father. "Next time you want to serve me, you can start by waking up early and bringing your happy butt into the kitchen to crack some eggs or mix some batter. On your way down, stop and grab your father and put him to work too."

My father cringed. "No, don't do that. Not unless you want trouble. I told your mother a long time ago. I don't cook. I don't bake. And I don't do chores. I got married so I wouldn't have to do that stuff. You know what I mean?" He winked at me as if I would agree with him and his chauvinistic beliefs. "All you need to do is focus on basketball. Make enough money to hire someone to do the cooking and cleaning." He patted my back before picking a pancake up with his fingers and folding it into his mouth.

I saw my mother narrow her eyes at him, but he either didn't notice or didn't care. He continued eating with his hands as he went on and on about the way he thought I should live my life. It never failed. All conversations went back to what he wanted for me, never on what I wanted. My hopes and dreams meant nothing to him. As long as he would come out looking like a hero, he didn't care about the details.

My mother served a plate for me and set it on the table. "Eat. You have a long day of studying ahead of you."

I opened my mouth to answer, but my father interrupted me.

"And basketball practice. He's got practice after class. Don't forget that," my father reminded us.

"I won't forget," I said. I looked at my mother. "Thanks for breakfast, Mom. You're the best."

She hugged me to her. "And don't you ever forget it. I'm your one and only Mama. How you treat me is how you'll treat your future wife, so keep saying please and thank you like I taught you."

I'd heard this speech before. It was a constant refrain between us. It was important to her that I know how to treat people. She always said, respect was earned. I had to show it in everything I did and with everyone I'd meet. In turn, I get respect back from them. That was a lesson I'd never forget.

CHARLIE

Finally, I can have my life back. Eleven years of living with my Aunt Jo is more than enough time to learn what I don't want or need in my life. If my mother was still here, I wouldn't have been forced to live in fear for my safety. I wouldn't have had to endure the pain and the long, lonely days of wishing she was still alive to hold me, to comfort me, to make sure no one – absolutely no one – ever put their hands on me or my twin sister Chloe. We deserved better than what we got. Now that I'm back in Chicago, I'm going to make sure I have the life I deserve to have.

"Oh my God! Look at you," Chloe exclaimed as I rounded the corner after exiting my flight. She pulled me in for the longest hug I'd ever experienced. I think we both needed to feel each other's heartbeats to confirm that this was real. We'd escaped the house of horrors. We were survivors. "I can't believe it's you. You're here." She finally pulled away from and hooked her arm through mine. "I can't wait to introduce you to everyone."

I shook my head at her because she was still the same old forgetful person she used to be when we were little. She'd forget the little things, but I had a hunch she'd never forgotten the horrible things we'd been through together. First, we had to watch as cancer ravaged our mother's body and then ultimately took her and sent our lives into a tailspin. Then, we were sent to live with our Aunt Joe and her husband Richard. They were supposed to be our saviors, the people who would protect us from wrongdoing and make sure that we were always well taken care of. They did neither of those things. Instead, they ridiculed us and demeaned us with their words and their actions until that wasn't enough, then, things became worse. So much worse.

"I don't know what you're talking about. I already know everyone I need to know is this life, and I don't even want to know half of those people," I joked.

She gave me the side eye. "Why do you do that? Why do you have to be so serious all the time? We're in Chicago. We're home. Everything is better here. Just wait and see." She glanced at my tattered suitcase. "Is that all you have?"

I nodded. "That's all that matters. As long as I'm far away from those people, life is good. What else do I need?"

She offered a coy smile. "Well, for starters, you need to do something with that hair." She and I giggled at the same time. It was just like the old days when we'd tease each other until we either burst out in loud, raucous laughter or got scolded for making so much noise.

It wasn't like Aunt Jo didn't make enough noise on her own. Between her and that sleazy Richard, I'm surprised either one of them could think straight. I didn't know which one was worse. They were both the most awful people I'd ever met. One did things I never wanted to speak of again and the other blamed us for the awful things he did to us. It didn't matter that we were her flesh and blood. All she cared about was that we behaved like obedient robots who smiled on cue and made her look good in front of her friends. Behind closed doors, she didn't care about us at all. In fact, it didn't faze her in the least to throw Chloe into the street like she was trash. Yes, she had a mouth, but who wouldn't after they'd lost their mother at such a young age?

As for me, after Chloe left, Aunt Jo turned her wrath at me. Not that it hadn't been there before, because it had. Somewhere not too deep below the surface, behind the cold stares and the pursed lips, were inklings of her true feelings for me. She didn't like me anymore than she liked herself. One thing I clearly remember my mother teaching us was that when people bullied you, it had more to do with how they felt about themselves – about the person in the mirror – then about the person they were directing their hatred toward. That's who my Aunt Jo was – someone who loathed herself, her situation so much, she took it out on everyone around her.

"So, if you're so happy to see me, you must have something fun planned for us? What is it? A nice, steak dinner with a side of baked potatoes, a salad and a biscuit, made from scratch? You know a girl has to eat?" I teased because we both knew neither one of us wanted to eat steak. This was Chicago. In this city, real people – not tourists – eat real food. We had it all. Chinese in China Town and everywhere else in the city and suburbs. The best fried chicken you'd ever eat at Harold's on the south side. Or we could grab a good old-fashioned Jimmy's Hot Dogs, no ketchup of course. The sky was the limit. With Mexican, Cuban, Jamaican, Italian, and every nationality in between operating businesses all over the city, Chicago was a food lover's dream and I couldn't have been happier to be home.

"We can stop and grab a slice of pizza before we hit the neighborhood, or we can stop at the grocery store and pick something up for you to cook for me. You know I don't have time to cook," Chloe said. "I don't know why you couldn't fly into Midway. It would have been a lot easier to stop at one of the pizza places on 63rd, instead of trying to find a decent place way out here in Rosemont.

I stopped walking and cocked a hip to one side. "Are you done?"

She arched a brow at me. "Done, what?"

"Complaining because you had to leave your little old apartment to pick me up at O'Hare," I teased.

She glanced around at the throng of weary passengers, who were waiting for their rides to come pick them up. "I'm done. Done with you already."

We stood eye to eye, challenging each other, but that only lasted for about five seconds before we gave into our laughter. This was part of the way we communicated with each other. We were so close, even though it had been a long time since we'd seen each other last, that we could tell what the other one was thinking.

She finally relented. "Let's go." She started walking toward Concourse C, in the opposite direction of our exit.

"Wait. Where are you going?" I asked.

She flashed her signature toothy grin at me. "What? You thought I drove here? Are you crazy? I'm not trying to get caught in airport traffic. I took the L, just like you're about to take. Hurry up so we can catch the Blue Line back." She didn't bother to see if I'd follow her. I had no choice. Walking to the city from the airport was a walk I never wanted to have to take.

When we reached the platform, it was wall to wall passengers, each carrying so much luggage, it made me wonder if how we'd all fit into the next train.

Chloe must have sensed what I was thinking because she grabbed my arm and whispered, "Don't worry. We're not standing on that train. I have a plan." She took my overnight bag out of my hands and pushed it up into her shirt. "See." She giggled.

I rolled my eyes. Yup, she was still the same girl I remembered.

"They'll give up a seat for a pregnant girl. Then, you can sit on my lap. Easy-peasy," she said.

We got on the train without incident. As hard as she tried to look like a pregnant girl, no one seemed like they cared too much about her safety. Like typical distracted commuters, they bumped into us, hit us with their suitcases, and got a little too close for comfort. The whole ride into the city was nostalgic. I remembered our mother carrying us everywhere on the bus or train. That's how we got around.

"What do you want to do after we eat?" I shouted over the loud thrumming of the train engine and chattering in the background.

Chloe grinned. "We're going out."

"Out where?" I shouted over the noise.

I noticed him the second I walked in. We locked eyes, but only for a second before some tramp started swinging her hips in front of him. He looked away for a moment to smile at me, then, turned his attention back to the girl.

"Oh, so you found him," Chloe said.

I shook my head. "Found who?"

She nodded toward the tall guy with the beautiful eyes. "The best-looking guy at the party."

"Whatever."

"Come on now, you don't have to deny your interest in Malcolm."

"I'm not denying anything thank you."

"Come with me so that I could introduce you to him."

"What? Oh, I don't think so. I will never give him or any other guy the opportunity to say that I'm thirsty. You can miss me with that Chloe."

"You're being over dramatic right now. I told you that I was going to introduce you to some people. Malcolm just so happens to be someone I want you to meet. He's one of the most popular guys at school."

"Do you two know each other?"

"Not really. I know of him, but I don't know him personally."

"Well Malcolm could introduce himself to me." Besides I don't want to meet him at this party maybe some other time. I don't want any drama. You see he's how that chick is all over him?"

"You don't have anything to worry about. Especially not Cici. She's that way with all the guys"

"Oh wow. If she likes it, I love it. I'm just here to have a good time. Now let's go tear up the dance floor."

Malcom

I learned a long time ago that most girls only hang around because they want something from you. I never considered myself a good catch. I'm alright. I'm smart enough. I can obviously play ball, but I'm not the best guy out there. I don't know what girls want and I don't have time to try to figure it out. I'm all about me and getting myself out of my situation soon. But when the sexy girl in the olive green fitted dress and nude stiletto heels walked in the door, everything I thought I understood about girls didn't match up to her.

Instead of eating up all the attention the guys were throwing at her, she was shy, almost nervous around them. While she looked good – great, better than any other girl I'd ever seen at one of these corny parties before – she didn't look like she fit in. Rather, we weren't worthy of her. She had class, long curly hair, style, a body that would make a grown man cry. She was different, and no one would ever be able to convince me of anything different. I was no expert, but I knew enough to know she was the only girl at this party I wanted to spend any time with, but first, I'd have to get rid of the ones who wouldn't stop climbing all over me, wishing and hoping I'd give them the time of day, so they could tell their little hungry girlfriends that they got a baller. I'm not trying to be nobody's baby's daddy anytime soon. I had better things planned for my future, but for right now, the only thing I had on my mind was that girl. Who was she and how could I get to know her better? I'd have to not come on strong.

Just as she noticed me, the skinny chic in front of me started gyrating like someone was paying her to do it. I glared at her to make her go away, mainly because she was blocking my view, but she didn't get the hint. Finally, I moved over to the side to get a better view. The girl in the dress glanced in my direction, but she didn't look happy to see me. Her eyes were on the skinny girl, who still hadn't gotten a clue. I had to move, and fast.

As soon as I gathered my courage and stood up, the DJ put on a song that got the crowd moving. I almost didn't make it to the other side of the room without getting trampled by swaying hips and waving arms and everything in between. The Lost Boys' music had that effect on everyone, including the pretty lady in the dress.

She was standing next to a girl who had to be her sister. They looked alike but carried themselves differently.

"Hi." In my haste, I couldn't think of anything sexier to say. I didn't want to scare her away.

She was swaying to the music. "Hi," she offered, a shy smile as she looked away.

"Do you like this song?" I asked.

She smiled. "I love the Lost Boys. Renee's Remix is a classic." She was into the music.

I held out my hand. "Dance with me?"

She looked at her sister, who urged her on. "Go ahead. If you don't, I will."

I hoped she'd agree.

"Sure, let's dance," she said finally, taking my hand.

I don't know if it was a figment of my imagination or wishful thinking, but I felt like the crowd made a path for me to guide this pretty lady on. They swayed and swung themselves off to the side to allow us to pass and take up a position in the middle of the make-shift dancefloor. Soon, everyone around us started singing along with the lyrics.

"Funny how love flies when we've just begun," we sang, everyone enjoying the music and the ones they were with. Most of them would probably never see each other again, but something told me, I'd do everything in my power to make sure I saw this girl again.

I wrapped my arms around her slim waist and pulled her closer to me. Not as close as I would have liked, but close enough to let her know I was interested. She blushed and looked away.

"What's your name?" I asked.

"Charlie," she answered, her voice sweet and tender like a cool breeze on a hot summer day.

"Where are you from?" I asked, wanting to keep the conversation going.

She looked at her sister, who was lost in the music on the other side of the room, dancing with someone else. "Here."

I did a double-take. I'd never seen her before. I would have remembered her if I had. "Are you sure?"

She giggled.

It was my turn to blush. "That was a dumb question."

The crowd's singing got louder, drowning out our conversation. I waited until the song was over and walked her over to a seat as far away from the DJ and people as I could find.

"Can I have your phone number?" I felt like a fool for asking. We hadn't even really had a conversation yet, but I was hoping we would soon.

She glanced over at her sister, who watched us like a guard dog, ready to attack if things went wrong. "Only if you give me yours too. I want to make sure you're not playing games with me."

I held my hand up in the air, palms out. "I wouldn't do that. If I'm asking for your number, it's because I intend to call you."

She grabbed my hand. "I'll put it in your phone as soon as you tell me your name."

Now I was really blushing. "Man, I suck at this. I didn't even tell you my name?"

"You didn't"

"My name is Malcolm"

"I already knew your name. I just wanted you to tell me."

Oh, I see. We both laughed.

MALCOM

"I'm leaving, Mom. Love you," I yelled as I passed by the entrance to the kitchen.

There she was, lying face up on the floor.

"Mom!" I dropped everything and ran to her. "Mom! Get up!" She didn't move. "Help!" Panic set in. I felt like my whole world had ended. "Help! Mom is unconscious! Help!"

I couldn't remember if anyone else was home. I was too distracted by all the good things going on in my life. I had the perfect girl, the perfect game, the perfect life and now my mother was lying unconscious in the middle of a room.

I dumped the contents of my backpack on the ground, searching for my cell phone.

"Where is it?" I yelled to no one as I kept one hand on my mom's shoulder. "It's going to be okay, Mom. I'm right here. I got you. It's okay." Then, I remembered. The cell phone was in my back pocket. I fished it out and dialed 9-

1-1. "Help me, please. My mom is passed out." The operator asked questions I couldn't answer. "I don't know," I shouted. "Help me!"

I stood outside the door of the Family Retreat waiting for the doctor to update me of the status of my mother.

"Are you okay?" Charlie ran up to me and wrapped her arms around me.

I'd never been so relieved to see someone in my life. "I'm okay. Thanks for coming."

She pulled away and noticed my father sitting there. "Hi. I didn't see you. How are you doing? Did the doctors speak to you yet?"

My father put on the charm for her. "She'll be fine. I'm sure we don't have anything to worry about."

I narrowed my eyes at him. What was he talking about? We had plenty to worry about. Nothing like this has ever happened before.

A nurse walked out from a bay of hospital rooms and said, "You can go in now."

I grabbed Charlie's hand. "Do you want to see her?"

She must have sensed my apprehension. "I'll do whatever you need me to do." She squeezed my hand.

We followed the nurse into my mother's room. She looked so peaceful, it frightened me. "Is she okay?" I asked.

The nurse nodded. "Yes. She's just resting. The doctor will come in and speak to you soon." She pulled a couple of chairs over from the other side of the room for us. "Here you go. Make yourselves comfortable. I'm sure she'll be thrilled to see you."

Within seconds of the nurse leaving the room, my mother opened her eyes. She seems me first. "Hey, there, my beautiful boy."

It was like I was a little boy again. I rushed over to her and wrapped my arms around her, emotion making me gasp for air. "Mom! You're okay?"

She hugged me back and kissed my cheek. "Of course, I am. I was just a little dehydrated, that's all." She saw Charlie and winked at her. "Thank you for coming, but I'm fine."

My father walked in the room, his head hung low. The smile vanished from my mother's face at the sight of him. They didn't say a word, but they didn't have to. It was evident there was something going on between them.

My mother had "tells." You knew that when she pursed her lips, she wasn't happy with you. When she squinted her eyes, it meant she'd had enough of whatever it was you were trying to say or do. When the little vein in the middle of her forehead made an appearance, that meant something very serious was going on.

As I looked at her now, helpless, lying flat on her back with tubes hooked up to machines, she displayed all three "tells" at once. It scared me. I'd never seen them all at the same time.

My father moved closer to her bed and reached for her hand. Her movement was subtle but spoke volumes about her mood. She pulled her hand out of his reach and smoothed her hair back.

"How do you feel?" he asked.

The look in her eyes was full of venom. She didn't answer. She didn't have to. A blind man could see how angry she was.

"Mom?" I tried. "Are you in pain?"

The doctor's eyes quirked up as we waited for her to respond.

She said, "I'm okay. I feel better now that you're here, Malcolm." She reached for my hand and squeezed it, just like she'd done a thousand times in my lifetime. Her anger wasn't directed at me.

"Do you need anything?" I asked.

She offered a passing glance at the others in the room. "No. Not right now. The doctor says I was just dehydrated."

I breathed a sigh of relief. "So, that's it? What happens now?"

She shot a glare in my father's direction. "I'll stay here to rest today while they give me fluids."

The doctor concurred. "Yes, we'll monitor her today and make sure nothing else comes up."

"Nothing else like what?" my father asked.

The movement was small, but powerful. Out of the corner of my eye, I saw my mother shake her head, as if begging the doctor not to say anything.

He cast his eyes down on the floor and cleared his throat.

"What is it?" I asked, a feeling of dread coming over me. "Is there something you're not telling us? How sick is she?"

My mother squeezed my hand again. "I'm not. I'm fine. I'm just tired." She yawned, but it seemed forced, like she was trying to signal for us to leave.

"Okay. If you're sure?" I asked.

She nodded. "Don't you have practice or something today?" She winked at Charlie. "Can you see to it that he does what he's supposed to do?"

Charlie nodded. "Yes, ma'am. I hope you feel better soon."

She grinned. "Everything will work out just fine."

The tone of her voice sent chills up my spine. What did she mean? What did she have to work out, and why was she so cold with my father? What had he done now?

A night without my mother in the house felt like the longest night of my life. The house was too quiet. Even with the TV on and music playing, the noise level wasn't normal. My father didn't come home until after I'd finally fallen asleep. He didn't even bother to say hello. I just happened to notice a light on in his room when I woke up this morning.

"Are you home?" I asked.

I heard shuffling in the room. "Yeah, you better get yourself going. It's almost time for school."

"I know. What about Mom? Are you going to go see her?" I assumed he would.

He opened the door and peeked out at me. "Not yet. She'll call me when she's ready. I have a meeting this morning." He promptly shut the door.

"You're going to a meeting when Mom is in the hospital?" I couldn't believe him. Why wasn't he going to be with my mom?

He opened the door again, his shirt open in front. "I saw her yesterday. She gets out today. I don't think a meeting is going to make any difference to her." He slammed the door shut.

I leaned on it and asked the question that had been bothering me all night. "Why is she mad at you?"

I could see his shadow under the door. He stopped moving when I asked. Several seconds passed by before he finally answered, "I don't know what you're talking about. Go to school."

"Hey, I heard about your mom. How is she?" Mrs. Lee my Precalculus teacher asked as I walked out of her class room.

"She's good. She's supposed to come home today." I didn't offer any more than that. No one needed to know my mom's business. She'd tell them herself if she wanted them to know.

I got stopped three or four times as I continued down the hallway. Everyone wanted to talk. Everyone wanted to make a connection. I was the official "It" dude. I was going to be something, and everyone wanted to make sure I didn't forget them along the way. Little did they know, I hoped no one would ever forget me.

As I walked past the office, the secretary gave me a look.

"What's up?" I offered with a wave.

She shook her head, a confused look on her face. "Hi, Malcolm."

Then, I heard it. There were loud voices coming from my father's office. I stopped dead in my tracks. That wasn't just anyone yelling. That was Coach Jacobs. I'd recognize his voice anywhere. Second to my father, he was the only other man who'd ever yelled at me.

I glanced in the little window in the door. Both him and my father were nose to nose, screaming at the top of their lungs at each other.

I ducked to the side, so my father wouldn't see me watching them.

Coach Jacobs said, "Did you think I wouldn't find out? Do you think I'm some kind of sucker that I don't know what goes on in my own home?"

My father, a man who never backed down from a soul, pleaded with him, "It just happened. I didn't mean for it to go that far. You know how these things go."

My heart dropped into my stomach. What were they talking about? What just happened?

There was a rustling noise like one of them pushed the other. I peeked in the window again, my heart racing a mile a minute. Coach Jacobs had my father pinned up against the wall.

"You want her so bad? You don't even know who she is, do you? You have no idea what you're inviting into your life." He laughed a deep, sinister laugh. "Congratulations, fool, she's yours. You can have her and everything that comes with her."

I couldn't believe what I was witnessing. My father was having an affair with Mrs. Jacobs, my French teacher. I grabbed the doorknob, ready to confront him for stepping out on my mother, but the coach wasn't done yet.

He backed away from my father, a grin on his face, but anger in his eyes. "Did she tell you about her problem?"

My father shook his head, fright in his eyes as he brushed himself off.

"Don't worry. You'll find out soon enough. You'll get it too. One day, you'll be going along thinking you got it all together, then, you'll wonder why it hurts to breathe, why your throat feels so dry, why you stopped remembering things, then, it will hit you. You'll go to the doctor and tell them about the cold you can't get rid of," he said, adding a laugh at the end. "You know what that doctor will do?"

My father shook his head. "No."

"He'll tell you the same thing he told me," he said, his smile growing wider. "I'm sorry, sir, but you've tested positive for HIV."

My forehead hit the door as I started to collapse to the floor.

"What?" My father must have regained his courage. Soon the door opened and pushed me along with it. He looked down at me. "What are you doing here? Don't you have a class to get to?"

The coach forced himself through the open door and stormed down the hallway, never saying another word about their discussion.

"What did you do?" I asked, my words barely audible. "What did you do to my mother?"

A look of terror filled his eyes, but he covered it up almost as quickly as it had appeared. "I don't know what you're talking about, but I know you better get to class."

Coach Jacobs returns and swung so hard, I thought my father's head would fall into my lap when it hit him.

The school secretary screamed for help. Security guards came running down the hallway and grabbed me by the arms.

"No. Wait. It's not me. I didn't do anything," I protested.

The secretary told them that my father and the coach were fighting.

The guards stopped, shocked expressions on their faces.

One asked, "Is that true, Principle Forehand? Are you okay?"

My father scowled at him. "I'm fine. Take him. Get him out of here." He pointed to Coach Jacobs. "Get him out of my building."

The guards tried to grab him, but he pulled away from them and stormed toward the exit door, screaming, "She's going to give it you if you don't have it already. Enjoy your HIV." He walked out the door, laughing loud enough to make each of us cringe.

I don't remember standing up. I don't know if he helped me to my feet or helped me to class. The next thing I remember is Mrs. Jacobs standing over me at my desk.

"What's wrong, Malcomb? Are you sick? Do you want to go to the nurse's office?" she asked.

I could barely look at her. I'd known her for so long. She'd come to my house. She'd had coffee with my mother. They were supposed to be friends. Now she was the woman who had slept with my father and probably broken my mother's heart. She may have given my parents HIV without even knowing it. How was I supposed to sit in her classroom and act like nothing had just happened?

Security officers knocked on her classroom door and asked her to step outside. I took that as my cue to leave. I didn't want to be there. I didn't want to be anywhere near the school, the coach, or my father ever again.

"Where are you going Malcolm? Cici asked."

"Why do you care? I responded sarcastically."

"I do care, that's why I asked."

"Whatever." I said as I packed up my belongings and headed towards the door. Just as I thought that is was good to exit. I came face to face with Mrs. Jacobs.

Oh Malcolm, I'm so sorry she reached out trying to hug me.

"Don't touch me. I said."

"Watch your tone young man."

"You're a joke. You need to practice what you preach. You're always trying to give us advise on having morals, but you're around here having an affair with my father, possibly infecting him and my mother with HIV. You need help you hypocrite." The entire class was quiet you could hear a pin drop. I left out and headed home.

Malcom

"Tell me again." Bradley, my older brother, motioned for his girl and son, BJ, to leave the room so we could talk.

I wasn't a crier. In my family, with my father, you didn't do that. You didn't show emotion. You powered through whatever it was, or he'd shame you for showing weakness. However, when it came to my mother, all bets were off. My mother was the queen. We worshiped her, and she worshiped us.

"I don't know how to explain it any better. He's having an affair," I said. "The woman he's banging is one of my teachers." It almost hurt to say the words. "She has HIV. She gave it to her husband – the coach."

Bradley shook his head. "She got AIDS?"

"No, she has HIV," I said again. "It's not the same thing."

He waved off my concerns. "I know it's not the same thing. I'm just trying to understand what you're saying. If she has HIV, then, does he have—" He stopped, his hands on his head. "What about Mom? Does she?" He punched the wall.

I hadn't thought about that. What if our father had given our mother something? I rushed to the master bath and rifled through the cabinet and drawers to check my mother's medications.

"What's up? What are you doing?" Bradley asked as he stepped into the master bath.

"Checking her medications. What if that's what all these pills are for?" I hated to even think about it.

Bradley helped go through the bottles and Googled some of their names as I searched for the other medication names on my phone.

He stopped. "Wait. She's dehydrated? Did she tell you that or did the doctor tell you that?"

I wracked my brain to remember who said what. "I can't remember."

He grabbed me by the front of my shirt, his face inches from mine. "This is no time to punk out. Get it together. What did the doctor say?"

I shoved him away. "I don't know. Does it matter? How is that going to help? If Mom wanted us to know, don't you think she would have told us herself?" I resisted the urge to punch something. My family was falling apart and there was nothing I could do to fix it.

He looked me straight in the eyes. "He's gotta go."

I nodded. "Let's do what we have to do."

I need to talk to you both. My father said.

Well we don't want to hear anything you have to say. "You have to go. You can't be here no more, man," I said as my father walked in the front door, looking tattered and confused as he took notice of Bradley and his family standing behind me.

"What do you mean? Go, where?" he asked, his voice weak and raw.

Bradley yelled, "Get your stuff out of my mother's house. You have five minutes."

Years ago, before my brother left, my father would have gone after him with full force. Today, with his dirty secret out in the open, he was a broken man. He wouldn't win. Not today.

I stood my ground. "Now. You're not going to hurt Mom ever again."

His emotions played out all over his face and body. His jaw slackened initially, then, hardened as if he was preparing for battle, then, softened again as his shoulders slouched with resignation. "Fine. I don't need this. Not from my own kids."

BJ, my brother's son, repeated my words, "Now."

My father swallowed a large lump in his throat, sadness in his eyes as he took in the defiant scene. "If that's the way you want it, but don't come running back to me when you need something."

I balled up my fists. "I'll never ask you for anything. I don't need you. No one here needs you."

He sneered as he made his way up the stairs toward the master bedroom. "Is that what you think? Your mother needs me, and she knows it."

I wanted to punch him. I wanted to drag him down the stairs and make him pay for what he did to our family, but I couldn't. No matter what he'd done, my mother would never allow me to put my hands on him.

No one said another word until he dragged a bag out of the house and slammed the door behind him.

Bradley stood stalk still as he watched him load his car and drive away. "It's going to be okay," he said.

I shook my head. "How can it be? Everything is ruined. Mom is sick. He's gone. We don't have anything anymore."

He shook his head. "That's not true. We have each other. I'm right here. My girl and BJ are here. You're here. We all have to be here for Mom. She's going to need us."

"Yeah, but how are we going to pay the bills? You heard him. He's not going to help us," I said as the realization hit me. Our lives were forever changed by my father's stupid mistake.

Bradley shrugged it off. "You have a lot to learn. Here's your first lesson: You do what you do to take care of you and your family."

I shook my head. "And how am I supposed to do that? I'm in school. I don't have a job. All I have is basketball. College recruiters are looking at me, but that's not going to pay the bills. What about the house and Mom's medication and all the other stuff that has to be paid for around here?" I was feeling hopeless and my father had only been gone for less than ten minutes.

He motioned for BJ and his girl to come into the room. "You see them?"

I nodded.

"Ask them if I ever let them go without anything," he said.

I knew the answer. I didn't have to ask them. My brother loved them. He'd give his life for them. He must have sensed what I was thinking because he draped his arms over my shoulder and rubbed the top of my head.

"I got you. You don't have anything to worry about. I'll show you how to make money. Real good money. Mom will be okay." He snickered. "She'll be better than okay. Trust me. She'll never have to worry about anything again."

The day's events weighed heavily on me. On one hand, I wanted to believe that everything happened for a reason. It wasn't like my father had ever been a saint. We knew he had secrets. At least, I knew he had stuff to hide. I just didn't know what kind of stuff it was. I figured it had to do with his dealings with college recruiters. I thought he was trying to get in on what they were offering me. I never expected that what he was doing was hurting my mother, endangering her life with a woman – a woman I knew. What kind of man does that?

I took a deep breath to clear the tension out of my body. "Okay. How are we going to do this?"

Bradley snickered. "One step at a time. You just have to be willing to work hard, and more importantly, be smart. This isn't no kid's game. This is real life. If you want to see good money and live in a nice place, you're going to have to do things my way. No excuses."

I knew what he was getting at, but for the first time in my life, I wasn't resistant to aligning myself with his lifestyle, especially not if it meant my mother would be okay. Whatever I had to do to make sure she was well taken care of, I'd work my fingers to the bone to make sure it happened, even if it killed me.

CHARLIE

I can't believe it's been seven months since the night I met him. So much has happened. So many things have changed. I don't know why I didn't notice before—as it was happening—but now, looking at him as he pulls away from me and the world, I can see it very clearly. Malcolm has changed. His mood is darker. His eyes no longer shine brightly as if he could see his future as something special. I wish I could find the right word to explain his transformation.

The corners of his lips lift into a smile. He caught me looking at him again.

"Watch it before you hurt yourself with that," he teases.

I love it when he's playful like this. It reminds me of when we first met. He was surer of himself, confident that he could take on the world—because he could. No one ever through shade his way because everyone wanted to be. I just wasn't so sure he wanted to be himself anymore. Life had changed him. Maybe it was his mother's illness or his father's treatment of her or a combination of both, but somewhere deep down in his soul, he buried who he was and became someone I could barely recognize. I had to help him, and I had the perfect plan to remind him of who he used to be and what his real dreams are. I don't want to lose him. And I hope, he doesn't want to move on without me. I don't think I'd be able to survive without him in my life.

"Hey, baby, how you doing'?" He walked over and kissed me on the cheek. At least he hadn't stopped doing that.

"I'm good." I took a deep breath before hitting him with a question. Probably the most important question I'd ever ask. "What would you say if I invited you to come by the house tonight? Like for a real, cozy date? Just me and you."

His eyes widened. "I'd say to stop playing with me. What's the catch?"

I tried to hide my disappointment. "Why does there have to be a catch? Can't I just want to spend some time with my man? Or, I'm sorry, maybe you're not used to someone wanting to treat you like a king? I think it's kind of romantic."

He furrowed his brows for a second as if he had to think about it before answering. "Okay. One more question. Who is going to be there? I mean are we going to be alone?"

I breathed a sigh of relief. "That's two questions." I winked to show him I was just kidding. "But I'll give you a pass because you're so cute."

He laughed. "All right. All right. Don't make fun of me. That's no way to treat a king." He smoothed his hand over his chin. "So, for real, will it be just me and you?"

I hadn't quite worked out the details yet, but since I had him interested, I figured I could figure the rest out later. If all went well, I'd make sure we could be alone for a few hours. For now, I just needed him to believe me for now or my plan to reclaim our relationship would never work.

He offered a sly smile as if he'd been let in on the biggest secret in the world. He lowered his voice, whispering in my ear, "You mean, me and you?" He snickered. "All alone?" His eyebrow quirked up. I think he knew what I had planned, but I had to play it off like that's not what I meant at all. I wanted to surprise him.

I grabbed his hand. "Yes, we'll be all alone, but get your mind out of the gutter. I just want to talk."

He groaned. "Talk? We can talk right here. I don't have to go all the over to your place to do that." He laughed at the thought of it. "Talk now. Go ahead. I'm listening." He cupped a hand to his ear to tease me.

"Stop it. You know what I mean," I said. "I don't know how to say this any other way, but I feel like something has changed between us." I hoped I hadn't pushed things too far by saying that.

He stopped laughing and let out a long sigh. "A lot has changed." He hesitated. "But not with us. We're good."

I wasn't so easily convinced. I think we could both tell that something had shifted. I'm sure he could see that all was not well in his world, and that made things go wrong in my life.

"Will you just do this for me? For us?" I'd always told myself I'd never beg a guy for anything. I was stronger than that. That's what I believed, but love or whatever it is I feel for him had changed me too. I needed him to do this for us. He didn't know it yet, but I believed with every ounce of my soul that this would save our relationship. What happened tonight would prove once and for all that he meant the world to me and that I'd never abandon him, no matter what. I'd be his rock. He'd love me forever and I'd never let him walk through life alone.

"You're serious?" For a moment, I saw the same sweet, loving guy I'd fallen in love with. Behind the sadness in his eyes was the Malcolm I knew. It made me feel good about things for the first time in a long time.

"You look like you're in a good mood," I said as I opened the door for Malcolm.

He winked. "Do I? I wonder why that is?" He kissed me softly on the lips. "Maybe it's because my girl invited me over to spend some quality time together. What's not to love about that?" He walked in and peeked around to see if we were really alone. "Just us?"

I nodded. "Yes. I told you we would be."

He wrapped his arms around me and pulled me close. "Yes, but now I'm wondering why you just want to talk."

"Stop teasing me. I asked you over here for a reason," I said, feeling nervous about how things would go. I'd never been intimate with a guy before. I had several boyfriends, but I never loved them, not the way I love Malcolm. Unlike a lot of the girls I know, I wasn't the kind of person to give herself to just anyone. I wanted to wait for someone special, for someone I truly loved. Malcolm is that guy.

He smirked, heat in his eyes. "What's the deal? You don't want to just talk, do you?"

"Yes, I did." I couldn't even say it with a straight face. Lying wasn't something I could pull off well. I didn't like to do it, especially with him. Without saying another word, I took his hand and lead him to the back of my house.

He stopped me halfway down the hallway.

"What's wrong?" I couldn't keep my voice even. My nerves were getting the better of me. I hoped I wouldn't ruin our moment.

I watched his chest rise and fall as I pushed my bedroom door open. He hesitated at the door, taking in the room, the photos on the wall, my desk, the bed. His hand tightened around mine. He took the lead and lead me inside, kicking the door shut behind us.

"Charlie?" Chloe slammed the front door so hard, the whole house shook.

"Get up. Get up. That's Chloe." I jumped off the bed in a panic. My clothes were at the foot of the bed, trapped under Malcolm's feet as he scrambled to get his pants on.

He tripped over his shoes and fell to the floor as the sound of Chloe's footsteps grew closer.

"I know you're here. Your purse is downstairs," Chloe said. "What are you up to?"

I jumped back into my bed and pulled the blankets up over me. "Don't come in here. I don't feel well. I think I'm coming down with something."

Malcolm grabbed everything off the floor, including my clothes and ran into the closet to hide, just as Chloe barged in the door.

"Don't you know how to knock?" I yelled, panic making me trip over my words.

She narrowed her eyes at me. "You think you're slick. I'm not stupid. Where is he? I know he's here."

"Who?" I feigned innocence. "I don't know what you're talking about. You can get out of my room now, though."

She shook her head and walked over to the closet doors.

I knew what she was about to do, but I still hoped that she wouldn't.

"Don't!" I yelled as she yanked the door open and exposed Malcolm, crouched down in the closet, completely naked.

She turned to face me a combination of a smile and a scowl on her face. "I knew it. You can't hide anything from me." She locked eyes with him. "Get dressed and get out of here. The party is over."

I wanted to crawl into a whole and die. I couldn't believe how quickly the night had turned ugly.

She stopped before she walked out the door, gave me a sinister look, then, looked at Malcolm. "You know what? Stay. You can finish. I don't want anyone to ever say I ruined Charlie's first time."

Charlie

I know I shouldn't let it bother me, but it does. Three days have passed since the night I invited Malcolm over and I haven't heard from him. Not only that, but I haven't seen his face once. I've heard everyone talking about him, like they always do, so I know he's been around. He just hasn't been around me, and that doesn't feel right. It's like he's avoiding me, and I don't know why.

It's not like I haven't tried to contact him. I've texted him, called him, waited for him in the hallway and he's never there. It makes me wonder what I did wrong. Did Chloe embarrass him so much that he feels like he needs to stay away from me?

One of my classmates, a girl I barely know, has been giving me the side eye for days. Every time I walk by her, she pulls a face like I did something to her. I don't know if she'd ever done that before, but ever since my night with Malcolm, things at school have been strange. She's everywhere. I can't turn around without seeing her face. She always stands with a group of girls. I don't really know them either, but I've heard about them. They're like a little clique of fast girls who think they can get any man they want just because, from what I heard, they're really quick to lay down with anyone and everyone.

I walk past her now and try to keep my eyes focused in front of me, but in my periphery, I can see her watching me, shaking her head at me like she's disappointed.

"Can I help you?" I ask as I make my ways to the stairs.

Her eyes go wide as if she's impressed by my reaction. She flashes a fake smile at me and waves me off. "Nope. There's nothing you could do for me. I can take care of your own."

How was I supposed to respond to that? I already have enough on my mind. I don't have time to deal with her drama. I chose not to respond and keep moving forward, hoping I'll run into Malcolm before the day was over. Maybe everything was just a misunderstanding and he's not been avoiding me. Maybe something else has happened at home.

After the final bell rings and I get ready to head home, my cell phone vibrates. I drop everything to pull it out of my back pocket and read it. It's a text from my friend Tamia.

"There's a party tonight. You HAVE TO come with me. I won't take no for an answer."

Tamia was a good person. She liked to take care of people. I knew what she was trying to do. She wanted to cheer me up, but I wasn't sure I was in the mood for a party. What did I have to celebrate? I'd slept with

Malcolm and never saw him again. That wasn't cause for celebration.

"Please," she texts.

"Fine, but I refuse to dance. I don't feel like it," I text back to her.

Music is bumping. The place is packed. I'm not sure I'm up for this, but I go in anyway because Tamia is so excited, and I don't want to disappoint her.

Heads bopping. Hands in the air, swaying to the music. I let out a sigh to rid myself of some of the tension, then, I saw him. My heart lodged in my throat as I realized he wasn't alone.

Tamia turned to face me, a shocked expression on her face. "Let's go."

I couldn't move. The world stood still. The only thing I could see was Malcolm and his ex-girlfriend Gina, their lips locked.

Tamia grabbed my arm and pulled me toward the door. "Come on."

I jerk my arm out of her grip and head straight for them. I yank Malcolm's arm. He turns, his mouth partially open. He's breathless.

Gina licks her lips and stands back, folding her arms in front of her as if she's just eaten a satisfying meal. The corners of her lips push up into a genuine smile.

"Charlie? What are you doing here?" Malcolm asks as he reaches for me.

I jerk away, my anger boiling. "What are you doing? After everything, this is how you show your appreciation?"

He responded, but the music drowned out his words as I stormed out of the room and ran outside. How could he do that to me? What did I do to deserve that?

As far as I'm concerned, our relationship is over. Gina can have you.

"Come on. Let's go." Tamia said.

"I'm not going to let him off the hook that easy, I responded." I threw the cup of fruit punch in his face and made my exit.

MALCOM

I know I hurt her, but I never meant to. I'm not that guy. Gina was my past. I never asked for her to come back into my life. I wouldn't do that, especially not to Charlie. She was my everything, but I have a lot going on. I never talk about it because I still don't know what it is.

Lately, it's felt like my whole world has crumbled to pieces and I wasn't sure how to put the pieces back together. She knows some of what happened, but she doesn't know the whole story and I'm not sure I want her to. My family problems are difficult enough without having to drag her into the middle of them. She doesn't deserve that. I'm a man. I'm supposed to handle things on my own, but that doesn't change the fact that I miss her like crazy.

I can't stop thinking about her. I don't know why I've avoided her. I feel ashamed for doing it, but now the time is right to make amends. I want to see her. I want to hold her. I want to love her like I should. I just hope she still feels the same way about me. What I did was dirty, and I'll spend the rest of my life trying to make it up to her, I swear.

Right before the last class lets out, I make my exit. The teacher doesn't care. Around here, most people let me get away with whatever I want. Lucky for them, I never take advantage of their kindness. I just want to get this right. If I can convince Charlie that I never meant to make her feel bad, then I'm halfway home. At least that part of my life will be right.

She has to come to her locker to get her stuff. I know she'll be here. I try to pull my thoughts together as I wait.

When Charlie bends around the corner, she takes my breath away. No girl has ever made me feel that way before. No girl does to me what she does. I know I'll never find another one like her either. She's a keeper.

It takes me a minute to realize what she's wearing. I've never seen her dress like that before. A form-fitting dress that hugs her in all the right places is a big change for me to take. She looks amazing, but it also makes me a little jealous. I don't want some other guy checking her out.

Chloe and her friend Tamia are with her. As soon as they see me, they catch an attitude. Apparently, they're not too happy with the way things went down between us either. I couldn't blame them for wanting to protect Charlie, but at the same time, I didn't think I owed them an explanation. The only person I wanted to speak to was Charlie.

They stepped in front of her as if to block my view of her. I knew what would come next. They wanted to argue with me about it.

Charlie moves out in front of them and bounds in my direction, anger oozing off her as she approaches. "Why are you here? What do you want?" she asks.

I'd never backed down from anyone in my life, but this little curvy thing with the cute curls made me want to run and hide. I said meekly, "I want to talk to you to tell you how sorry I am—"

She cuts me off with a wave of her hand. "No. You don't get to talk to me after what you did. You used me once. I won't let you do that again." She didn't even bother to step over to her locker and grab her things. Instead, she pushed past me, followed by her snickering girls.

I attempted to get her attention, but it appeared that my teammate Johnathan beat me too it. The way the two of them were looking into each other eyes bothered me. I've never seen Charlie with another man. Yet alone look at one the way that she's looking at him. As bad as I wanted to interrupt their conversation. I let them be. If it's meant to be, we'll be back together in no time. I guess only time will tell.

CHARLIE

I tried to resist. I wanted to. I think. I thought if I made him wait, he'd realize that he needed me as much as I needed him, but my heart wouldn't let me completely walk away from him. We're too invested in this. I'm too invested in us. As much as I hate to admit it – I'll probably regret it someday – he's everything to me. There's no one else in school or anywhere else in this world, I'd like to spend any time with. He's it for me. That's why I had to take him back.

"You can say it, you know?" he whispers into the phone.

I blushed even though he couldn't see me. "I can say what? I don't know what you're talking about?"

He snorted. "Yeah, right. You don't know. I thought you knew everything. Isn't that what you told me?"

I covered my mouth with my hand to hide my laughter. He was right. I had told him a dozen times how smart I was. I told him I knew everything he was thinking even before he started to consider it. We were that close. At least that's what I told myself.

"You're not funny," I said, despite my laughter.

"Then, why are you laughing?" he teased.

I checked the time. We'd been on the phone for over an hour and I still hadn't started dinner or done any of my homework.

"I'm laughing at you, not with you," I said as I turned the knob on the oven to turn it on.

His end of the call went silent.

"Are you still there?" I laughed because I knew he wouldn't hang up on me, especially after all we'd been through. "I hope you're not pouting."

He chuckled. "I'm here. I was just thinking. I do that sometimes."

Something was up. His attitude completely changed.

"Let's not do this right now. Just say what you have to say." I swallowed hard, fearing he'd give me bad news. "It's not about us, is it?"

His end of the line went silent again, like he'd covered the phone.

"Malcolm?" I could feel my heartrate increase as I asked. "Please tell me."

"Just a second, okay?" I heard him put the phone down and walk away.

I listened intently, trying to figure out who or what had him so distracted.

He returned sounding happier. "Do you think you can get out tonight?"

I glanced at the oven. I still hadn't pulled anything out of the freezer to cook. "Not really, but you can come over if you want."

"I'll be there in fifteen minutes." He hung up.

Sure enough, Malcolm arrived just as he said.

I almost couldn't breathe. "What did you say? Don't play with me now."

Malcolm wrapped his arms around me. "Yes or no?"

"This weekend? Where are we going?" I asked.

He let out a long sigh. "Will you, please, just trust me? You'll ruin the surprise."

I hated to be that girl, but I didn't feel comfortable agreeing to anything unless I knew what I was getting myself into. Malcolm hadn't been himself lately. It was like he was always on guard, distant. He tried to act like everything was normal, but there was plenty of indications that something was going on with him.

He kissed the top of my head, whispering, "Please, I need you to do this... for us."

"Surprise," he said as the limo he rented for us pulled up in front of the Chicago Langham Hotel & Resorts.

I looked from him to the doorman and back at him. "Are you serious?"

He smiled from ear to ear. "Trust me?"

I jumped into his lap and kissed him like I'd never kissed him before. "Yes. Yes. Yes."

The driver opened our door. "Enjoy your stay."

The doorman signaled for a bellboy to grab our bags. "Welcome to the Langham."

I gulped. "I can't believe you did this. How did you know I've always wanted to stay here?"

Malcolm winked at me. "I pay attention."

We stepped into the elevator. I still couldn't believe any of this was real. When we signed in, I kept pinching myself to make sure this wasn't a dream.

Malcolm grabbed my hand. "I want to do something before we go up to the room."

I didn't know if I could take any more surprises. "Okay. What is it?"

He pulled a small box out of his coat pocket. "I want to give you this."

I gasped as he opened the box. "What is that?"

He blinked back tears. "It's a promise ring. I promise that I'll never, ever hurt you again. I promise I'll never do anything to make you feel bad. To prove that, I want you to have this and wear it every day to remind you of how much you mean to me."

"You... you..." I couldn't get the words to leave my mouth.

"Here's another promise. When we turn eighteen, I'm going to marry you. You can count on that, so don't bail on me. This is for real. We're in this for the long haul."

I couldn't contain my emotions anymore. I jumped into his arms and cried happy tears.

When the elevator stopped on our floor, he held the door open. "Wait. You have to let me give you the ring."

I stared at it as we walked down the hallway and as he opened the door to our room. When I looked up, I saw the most beautiful room I'd ever seen. Dozens of red and white roses welcomed us. Flower petals lined the walkway from the door to the bed to oval-shaped bathtub in the bathroom. He'd left no stone unturned.

Malcomb walked over to the nightstand and plugged his phone into a charger and played the song Joy by Blackstreet. He turned to me and said, "Dance with me."

Of course, I will. I replied. Malcolm went out of the way to make tonight beautiful. I couldn't have asked for more. He kept his word on doing all that he could to make it right with me. He knows he had to let his actions show, because I'm not the girl who you could just disappoint and then apologize. I like to see and feel your I'm sorry. I couldn't wait to share the great news with Chloe and Tamia. They were kind of leery about Malcolm and I getting back together. They were under the impression that Malcolm was jealous Johnathan and I had started dating. I felt that way too. However, I was still in love with Malcolm. I wanted my relationship back with him. And at the end of the day, love conquerors all.

Malcom

Nothing gives me more energy than to hear the roar of a crowd, excited and anxious to watch me play. I live for that feeling. Nothing can compare to it. I just wish my mother could be here to watch me play. It's the championships. I've worked hard the whole season to make it to this point, but, yet, she can't be here. Her health has continued to fail her. She doesn't deserve to be in the pain she's in. She tries hard. She tries to be strong, but I can tell. She's not doing well. Small parts of the woman she once was have begun to fade away. She's more tired than; she's dying. We've pushed that thought out of our minds, mostly to ease our own pain, but when we're alone at night, we know the truth. Our mother is dying and there's nothing we can do about it to make it stop.

"Let's get it," Johnathan my teammate said as he patted my back. "We got this."

I nodded, confident that we did have what it took to beat our competition. "Yeah, we got this. Let's suit up and get that championship."

We made our way down the corridor to the locker room. On the walls, enclosed glass cases showcased all the awards the school teams had won over the years. Right in the center was an empty space. I stopped to admire it, my reflection showing in the glass. That space was for the trophy they knew we'd bring home today. I swallowed a lump of emotion in my throat, both humbled by the confidence people at the school had in me and pride for all I'd done. I just hoped my mother would be around to watch her baby boy reach his biggest achievements.

"Why'd you stop?" my teammate asked as he held the door to the locker room open for me.

I shook my head. "I'm good. I'll be there in a minute."

He waved his hand, motioning for me to follow him. "Stop thinking about that girl and let's play ball."

The crowd cheered and clapped so loud the ground shook under our feet. I thought she was a figment of my imagination until Charlie wrapped her arms around me.

"Surprise!"

I gave her a quick squeeze, then, turned my attention to the real surprise and gently scooped my mother up in my arms. "You're here."

She smoothed her frail hand over my cheek. "I couldn't miss your big moment. And guess what? Your brother has decided to splurge. He's taking us all out to dinner."

I looked at the group. "Everyone."

My brother slapped my back. "Me, you, your girl, mom, and Angelo.

I nodded my hello to Angelo. He was one of my brother's friends.

We walked outside to a top-of-the-line Jaguar SUV.

I whistled at the vehicle. "Smooth, but we won't all fit in there. I'll ride with Charlie."

She smiled. Ever since I'd taken her away for the weekend, she'd relaxed. She stopped asking me a lot of questions. I think the weekend and the ring eased her mind, and I was glad. She didn't need to take on any more stress from me and my life.

I held Charlie's hand as I drove behind my brother. Everything was perfect. I had my girl, my mother had come out to watch me play, my team won, nothing could ruin this night.

I got lost in the moment until Charlie pulled her hand out of mine. "What are they doing? Who is that?" She pointed to a car that rolled up on the Jaguar at a stop sign.

I slammed on my breaks. Everything happened so fast. First, the glint of gun caught my eye. By the time I could react, shots had gone off as my brother gunned the gas on his vehicle. The Jaguar flew in the air and landed yards away into a ditch. The car with the shooters sped off. I didn't see which way they went.

"Slow down," Charlie said as I sped in the direction of the car, oblivious to stop lights and other cars on the road. I had to get to my family.

Smoke billowed from both ends of the vehicle. The front end was in shambles. The back hatch was open. As soon as I jumped out of the car, I could see how bad it was. Angelo's head was slumped forward, blood spewing out of his forehead. I rushed to the passenger seat to check on my mother.

"Mom? Mom! Mom!" I screamed.

Charlie ran up behind me and saw her. "Oh my God! Oh my God!"

I couldn't see straight. I couldn't think straight. They were dead. All dead.

"NO!"

"We're so sorry for your loss," someone said.

I didn't look up. I didn't make eye contact with anyone. I hadn't since the accident.

Someone touched my shoulder. I jerked away. "Get off me."

Charlie whispered, "Malcolm, they're just trying to comfort you. Don't do that."

I didn't want sympathy. I wanted revenge, but I couldn't tell her that. She didn't need to be a part of any of it. I'd already lost enough people I loved. I couldn't get her into this. I'd die protecting her.

Teachers, staff, my teammates, the coach all watched me like I'd done something wrong, like what happened was my fault. I knew I wasn't being rational to think that. No one truly blamed me, but I blamed myself. The whole family had come out to watch me play. It was my fault they were outside at all. It was my fault my mother had left her warm bed. Because of a stupid basketball game, my mother and brother and his friend were dead. I couldn't breathe when I thought about it. I couldn't get the images of their bloodied bodies out of my mind. It lived with me all the time. Every time I opened my eyes, I saw them. When I closed my eyes, I'd hear the pop, pop, pop of the bullets. I remembered the flash when the gun went off. Like small lightning strikes, they disappeared almost as quickly as they appeared. Those few seconds – three or four at most – will live with me for the rest of my life.

"Malcolm," Charlie urged as she tugged my shirt sleeve. "Did you hear me? Your fist is balled up. Please calm down. Maybe you should have stayed home today. I think you need more time."

I heard her, but I couldn't focus on her words. I had to stay focused. I didn't have it in me to want to make everyone feel better. That wasn't my job. I was the one who witnessed my brother, mother and friend be gunned down right in front of me. My pain wasn't up for debate. They didn't get a say in how I should react to their fake sympathy claims.

I sighed. "You're right. I shouldn't be here. I'll pick you up after school today. Meet me in front."

She said, "You don't have to do that. I can get home by myself."

I narrowed my eyes at her. She knew how I felt about this. I was paranoid something would happen to her. I couldn't let her walk home alone.

"Meet me in front after school. I don't want to argue about this," I said before I walked away.

My father stood in a doorway, laughing with one of the teachers. He stopped cold when he saw me.

"Son," he said.

I didn't look up. I couldn't look at him. I hoped to never see his face again.

"Malcolm," he called out after me. "How are you doing?"

My feet couldn't move fast enough. I had to get away from him before I said or did anything to him. As much as I hated him for what he did to my mother, to our family, I swore I'd never touch a hair on his head. Not out of respect for him because you have to give respect to get respect, but because my mother wouldn't want me to do anything to him. I'd stay clear of him for her.

"Whatever you need us to do, we got you," one of my brother's former lieutenant said. "It's all you now."

I leaned forward, elbows on the table. "I want them to pay for what they did. I want to hurt them."

The group nodded their heads. They understood what I meant. I didn't have to spell it out for them. They knew how the game worked. An eye for an eye. More lives would be lost, and I didn't care. As long as it didn't touch me and my people, I was fine with living with the consequences.

"Who do we hit first? You want us to take whoever we find out or do you have a list of targets?"

I'd spent the last few days thinking about how I wanted to handle this. I refused to kill innocent people. No one should ever suffer like my mother did for something she had no part of. I wouldn't do that to another family, but I would have a guilty party pay for what they'd done.

I nodded. "I have a list."

They waited eagerly for me to continue, but I needed a minute to make myself right with my decision. I couldn't allow any mistakes to happen. It had to go according to plan, otherwise my mother and brother's lives would have been for nothing. That's not what I want. I want people to remember who they were. I want them to know my mother for the innocent angel she was. She never hurt anyone. Her whole life was our family, and ironically enough, the family killed her. My father's cheating and lying broke her heart. His sleeping around made her sick, sick enough to kill her slowly. Life, the situation my father forced us into, finished the job. I had to make it right. I'd never be able to bring her back. I'd never get to see her face again or hear her voice again, but hopefully, a small part of the pain would wither away, and I couldn't make it through another day.

"Well? What do you want to do first? How is this going to play out?" Keon asked.

"Tye. We get him first," I said.

"Tye?" Keon responded. "That will be a big hit. You sure you want to start with him."

I tried to recall the image of the man I saw with the gun in his hand. I had no doubt in my mind Tye was the shooter.

I nodded. "He killed my family. Now, he has to go. Execution style. Make an example out of him. No mercy. No time to scream or cry or whine. Make it happen. I don't care how or when. Just do it."

"Execution style?"

I nodded as I pulled an image up on my phone. "This is his house. He lives here with a couple of his guys. This is where you get him."

"His mom lives around the corner from me. That would be easier. He's over there every morning," Keon said.

"No," I said. "Not in front of his mother. Get him at his place. That's where he handles his business. That's where he needs to die. We'll make an example out of him if we play this right."

"If that's what you want."

I snickered. "Do you want to know what it is that I want? Do you really want to know what this list is all about?" My blood boiled as I thought about what I'd been through. "This is about me taking over the operation. This is about making it known that I can't be stopped. This is me reaching the top by any means necessary. This is my big move."

"Then, when he's gone, what do you want us to do?"

They had no idea this was only the beginning of what I had planned to become the youngest kingpin in Chicago. Tye was only one run on the ladder to my success.

"I want Eternal Revenge. This is only the beginning," I said.

"I'm about to pour out my wrath on the city of Chicago. The responsible ones that it."

"The streets know that there will be consequences. I think we should wait before we make a move. As soon as they think that everything has blown over. That's when we strike a match." Keon said.

"I actually like that idea. Therefore, I'm making you my underboss. I like how you think. This right here, we're family. We are all we got. Anyone outside of us, can't be trusted, unless proven otherwise. We must move smart out here. One mistake can cost you your life."

"My brother was not the violent type. He was way more trust worthy than I was. He ran his business smoothly which is why no one will ever find a mug shot or any criminal charges filed against him. Things are about to change."

"I don't think that it's a good idea to go to war. Especially not right now, while the elections are going on. We don't need that heat." Johnny said.

"Were you not listening to anything Keon and I said?" I replied.

"Yeah. I just feel that we should wait until at least the mayoral elections are over with." Johnny added.

"Everyone listen up. Don't anyone make any moves until I say so. Keep your eyes and ears open always. Of course, you know business must proceed as usual. If you have any problems, contact Keon. He will then contact me. Now let's wrap this meeting up. I have to get home to my girl."

"What are you in love now." Johnny asked playfully.

"Without a doubt." We all laughed which was good for me because I haven't laughed in what seems like forever.

Malcom

"Nah, I can't let you do that."

Charlie cocks her head at me. "What do you mean you can't let me? In case you forgot, I'm not your child. The last I checked, you didn't have any children. Unless there's something you want to tell me, you better apologize."

I hated when she did this. She didn't do it very often. She was a good girl, but she also had a fire in her that would come out every now and then. She drew the line and became defensive when she thought I was telling her what to do. The thing was it was my job as her man to protect her. If that meant I had to hear her complain, then I was okay with that.

When I didn't respond immediately, her attitude grew ten-fold. This time, she added her pouty lips to the mix. That got me every time. She knew I'd fall for it too. I could tell by the look in her eyes.

"Fine. I'm sorry, but—"

She waved her hand in my face. "But nothing. I'm going to Lollapalooza whether you like it or not. It's not fair that you get to go out and hang out with the guys. I don't remember you asking me how I felt about that. Now, you want to sit here and act like I can't go and hang out with my girls."

I'd had enough. It was clear she'd taken what I'd said the wrong way. "Charlie, listen to me. I didn't say you couldn't go. I just said it wasn't happening. There's a difference."

"What's the difference?"

I stifled a laugh because she was so cute when she was being unreasonable.

Since the pout worked so well for her, I thought I'd give it a shot. "I want you to come with me. All of you. It will be fun. What do you say?"

Her eyes lit up. She was into it, but her stubbornness wasn't ready to let me have my moment. "Oh, so now you want to act like you have a girl?"

I held my face tight. If I laughed, we'd start this argument all over again. It was better to let her think jealousy was why I didn't want her to go without me, but the truth was, I was terrified. She was all I had left in this world. The streets of Chicago are hot. If something ever happened to her, I don't know what I'd do. I couldn't let her out of my sight. I could keep her safe.

I don't know what was going on in her head, but whatever it was calmed her down. She looked at me coyly and said, "You want me to go with you? That's so sweet."

"Yep," I said as I breathed a sigh of relief. At least I wouldn't have to worry about her safety.

"Oh, no, no, no. What is this?" I grabbed her hand and spun her around. She was drop-dead gorgeous from head to toe. Nothing was out of place. In fact, everything – her curves, her slim waist, her sculpted arms and shoulders – were there for the world to admire, and that made me both proud because she was all mine and nervous because every other guy in the park would have their eyes on her too.

"What's wrong with the way I look?" She blushed at the way I was looking her up and down. "You don't like our cute outfits? We match. We haven't done that in so long?" She pulled Chloe toward her. Both were dressed exactly alike in form-fitting hip hugger jeans and short, revealing crop tops. I couldn't let that fly... unless I kept Charlie by my side.

Marsha their friend fluttered around, all attitude and almost nothing else. "Hey! What about me? I look good too, you know?"

I hadn't noticed. She wasn't someone I kept on my radar. I nodded to acknowledge her and feed her ego a little but didn't say anything to upset Charlie or to get anyone thinking anything I didn't want them to. Girls loved to do that kind of thing. They always made something out of nothing and I wasn't interested in any of that nonsense. I was here to enjoy the concerts, not get caught up in some new drama. I'd had my share of that already and it almost broke me.

The first group got on stage. The crowd started hooting and hollering. The vibe was good. I could finally relax and enjoy some time with my girl and friends. It was a nice distraction from everything else... for now.

A sudden chill came over me. Something wasn't right. I could feel it in my bones. There was something up. I already had Charlie in my arms, but my gut instinct told me to hold her closer, to protect her, but I had no idea where the threat was or what it would be.

"What's up?" Ernest, a member of my crew, leaned toward me, speaking low so Charlie wouldn't hear him.

I turned my head away from Charlie. "You feel it too, right? Keep your head up. I think someone scoped us out."

Just then, a serious of pops broke out. This was Chicago. Most people were familiar with that sound. As if it was a movie I was watching on a big screen and not happening in real life, I watched it happen in slow motion. First, the pops. Then, a quiet murmur in the crowd. That swelled into agonizing screams and mayhem as they slowly began to realize what the noise was. Instinct kicked in for me. I grabbed Charlie and threw her down to the ground and jumped over her, shielding her from the hail of gunfire. Flashbacks about the day my mother and brother were murdered in cold blood flooded my mind.

Charlie began to cry uncontrollably.

I comforted her as best as I could, but with the anger building up in me on top of the rage I'd held in my heart since the last incident, my words didn't soothe her. She trembled under me like a scared puppy and I could do nothing to make the fear subside. The only thing I could focus on was the sound of the bullets, the fear in the voices of those scrambling for their lives, and the hatred I had in my heart.

My guy, Ernest, collapsed next to us, bleeding out.

Charlie screamed in horror.

I reached for him to cover his wounds and stop the bleeding while Charlie clutched the front of my shirt, begging me not to leave her.

"No, please, don't leave me. Please, don't go," she pleaded. "Don't leave me here."

It broke my heart to hear her say those words. The last thing I'd ever do is leave her alone. She was my rock. My everything.

Before I had a chance to respond and tell her that I'd never leave her, Chloe screamed a gut-wrenching scream and fell to the ground next to Ernest.

"Oh, my God!" Charlie yelled. "She's been shot. She's been shot!"

Adrenaline kicked in. I wanted the shooter dead. I wanted everyone who'd had anything to do with this and with my brother and mother's death to pay with their lives.

I grabbed Chloe with one arm and lifted her over my shoulder, while pulling Charlie to me. "I got her. I got her. It's going to be okay."

I don't know if either of them heard me over their hysterical cries. I'm not sure I'd said anything aloud. The only thing I was sure of was that someone would die tonight, and it wouldn't be anyone I cared about. That would never happen again if I had anything to say about it.

"Ernest let's go. We have to get out of here, man." I nudged his leg, but he didn't move. "Ernest!"

The crowd was still going wild. Security and police flanked the stage as the performers scrambled to get out of the line of fire, but I knew they weren't the targets. We were.

I didn't have to touch him to know he was dead. I did anyway. "Ernest, get up, man. Get up."

I could feel eyes on me. I didn't care about the people in the crowd. I didn't care about the security guards or the cops. Joe Austell and his crew were there, somewhere. They did this.

"Malcolm," Charlie said as she tried to pull me back. "Don't. Please, don't. Whatever you're thinking about doing, don't."

Lying wasn't my forte. I didn't like to do it, but in this instance, I had to shield her from the truth, so she wouldn't get hurt. "Go with your sister to the hospital. I'll meet you there."

She shook her head. "No. Come with us."

"Go!" I said it as firmly as I could without scaring her. "Please. I'll meet you there, I swear."

The sight of Ernest lying in a pool of blood made me sick to my stomach. Anger turned to rage. Rage turned to hate. Hate made me move. Someone had to die for what they did. Someone is going to pay tonight. This will not go undone mayoral elections or not.

Malcom

"What's the word?" Tan asked.

"They took care of Laz. Tortured and killed him just like what I plan to do with Joe," I said as I pulled the car onto Joe's block. I had a clear view of his ramshackle house, complete with a yard full of discarded bottles of beer and every brown paper sack in the city. He lives like the piece of garbage he is. I'd do the world a favor by getting rid of him for good.

"You want us to handle this?" Tan asked.

I didn't have to say a word. They understood how things were going to go down.

Boogie crouched low and moved fast as he approached the house. Tan did the same behind him. Both dove under the house, waiting for their opportunity to strike as soon as Joe walked out the door.

I hitch my breath when I see that front door open. This is it. He dies now. Boogie and Tan came from under the house running up on Joe. I can't hear what they're saying, but I can tell by the way Joe moves that he must be trying to talk himself out of the situation.

I slip out of the car. I want to hear this fool beg for his life. I didn't have to go far to hear him. He blamed the whole situation on Paul, a well-known and respected kingpin – my brother's best friend.

He hasn't seen me yet, and that's good because I can't breathe. I can't think straight. I go for cover in my car just as the shooting begins. Two AR-14 rifles take aim at him and fire in rapid succession. Boogie and Tan laughs at the flipping of Joe's body part, as they take turn pulling their triggers. I don't feel anything. Not like I expected. I hoped for some sort of relief, a sign that the pain would go away, but watching him die didn't give me that.

They jumped in the car and I drive off before anyone knows what happened.

"He said Paul did it," Tan said. "He blamed him for everything. Did you hear him, Boogie? He was begging and crying like a—"

"No! It wasn't Paul!" I slammed my fist on the steering wheel. I refused to believe he'd do my brother like that. They were boys, partners. He wouldn't betray him.

"So, you think Joe was lying?" Tan asks.

"Yes," I said.

Boogie shook his head. "No. I don't think so. You should've seen the look in his eyes. He could have said anyone's name, but he said Paul's. Why him of all people? That doesn't make sense. Why would he lie?"

Tan nodded. "Yeah, I don't think he'd lie."

I took the next corner at a quick clip, tires squealing.

"Look, man, all I'm saying is I think you should find out for yourself. You don't want to go through life with that hanging over your head, especially if you plan to take this all the way."

All I could think was about how quickly my life had changed. Not so long ago, I was a basketball star, well on my way to fame. The next, I'm this – a gangster, making my own rules, calling the shots, and out for revenge. If it turns out that Paul had anything to do with it, he'll pay. For now, I have to keep him away from Chloe, or worse, separate Charlie from her sister to keep her safe.

CHARLIE

I was ready for this to be over. I just want our lives back.

A knock at the door catches us off guard as we're getting ready to leave the hospital.

"Hello. I'm Detective Allen. Do you have a minute to talk?" he asks Chloe.

She gulps.

"Do we have to do this right now? She's been through a lot. We just want to take her home," I try to persuade him.

His gaze falls to her bandages. "Yeah, sure. No problem, but just so you know, we can't find the person who did this, if you don't talk to us." He offers a smile and hands her a business card. "When you're up to it or if you remember something, you haven't already told officers, give me a call. Day or night." He turns to leave and stops to chuckle when he sees Paul at the door. He looks over his shoulder at Chloe. "Popular place. Everyone who is anyone is here." He narrows his eyes at Paul and walks away shaking his head.

I wasn't worried about the detective. My concern was Malcolm. He'd grown colder since the incident at Lollapalooza.

Chloe lights up when she sees Paul walk in the room. Malcolm's fist clench at the sight of him.

"Malcolm, I want you to meet my boyfriend," Chloe says.

He smiles, but I can tell it's not genuine. It's almost diabolical. "Nice to meet you, Paul. Could I have a word with you alone?"

Paul doesn't say a word, but he follows Malcolm out of the room.

"What's up with that?" Chloe asks. "They know each other?"

"What's wrong?" Malcolm asked.

I hesitated to tell him, but after all that's happened, I hated to hold anything back. "Promise me, you won't go crazy. It's probably nothing."

"Talk," Malcolm urged me.

"A car has been following me." He lurched forward, throwing the Maserati into overdrive.

"Who? In the Porsche?" he asked.

"No. I haven't been driving that. I don't know who it is."

He went quiet, but I could practically see the wheels in his head turning. The way he'd been acting lately, I knew he wouldn't let this go.

"Malcolm?" I urge.

He shook his head. "No, not now. This is what's going to happen. It's time for you to move in with me. I told you this a long time ago and let you talk me out of it, but I'm going to put my foot down on this. You can't be alone anymore. It's not safe. You're moving in and that's it."

His tone scared me. I knew better than to respond before he had time to cool off. I sat back in my seat and waited for his breathing to slow down. It took thirty minutes of driving around the city before I felt safe enough to say anything to him.

"Can we talk now?" I asked.

"Can it wait? I want to do this first," he said as we pulled up to The Sinclair. "Let's go inside and officially welcome you to the penthouse."

"What penthouse? Who lives here?" I'd never seen the beautifully ornate building before. At least not in recent memory.

He smiled, reminding me of the old Malcolm, the one I fell for not so long ago. He could tell by the twinkle in his eye that he needed to do this. "We do," he said. "But you can't tell anyone. Not even Chloe."

I understood his reasons, but that didn't mean I had to like cutting my sister off from this part of my life. I wanted things to go back to the way they used to be. I wanted my nice, safe life with Malcolm, not the one where every moment is filled with uncertainty and his every move was dictated by forces outside of our control.

"Are our lives in danger?" I asked as I looked around our place. Everything was gorgeous. It was in stark contrast to what our lives felt like lately.

"Yes. That's why no one can know we live here."

"But—" I couldn't get the words to come out as my emotions spilled over. "I... I ..." I swallowed my sorrow and said, "We can't leave my sister out there by herself. She should be here with me. We should be together. She's all I have."

He gulped.

"I mean, you and Chloe are all I have in this world."

He nodded. "I know, but you have to trust me on this. Everything will work out. I promise."

So much is going on and is happening so fast. I hope things change for the better. I refuse to live my life in fear, being followed, etc.

I punched in Chloe's cell number to check up on her. I just needed to hear her voice and know if she's okay. Malcolm may not like it but I'm going to do all that I can so that Chloe is here with me. Some day he will understand.

"Are you comfortable? Malcolm asked."

"Yes. How could I not be?"

"Good because I going to step out for a minute."

"But can this wait? I want you here with me."

"No. I'm sorry love. I'll be back soon."

"Okay. You be careful." We share a kiss.

I Yarn while flipping through the channels, hoping to catch a good movie, as I waited for Malcolm to come home.

Charlie

The next morning there is no sign of Malcolm. I didn't know what to think. I hope that everything is okay with him.

After devouring the breakfast I'd prepared for the both of us, I loaded the dishwasher. I return to our bedroom to get dressed. I'm meeting Chloe and Jade.

"Happy Birthday, baby," Malcolm said as he wrapped his arms around me.

"Aw, thank you." I tried to turn to kiss him, but he pulled away. "Let me kiss—" I stopped when I saw him. He was down on one knee.

"Marry me, Charlie," he said as he placed a small box in my hand.

My hands shook as I opened it. Inside was the most beautiful ring I'd ever seen. My eyes filled with happy tears. "It's... It's..."

He stood up and placed the ring on my finger. "It's a custom canary yellow diamond. I hope you like it. I snuck out of the house this morning to meet with the jeweler. I wanted to surprise you on your birthday."

I jumped up and down, giddy with excitement. "I love it. I love you. Oh, my God! Is this for real? You want to marry me?"

I jumped into his waiting arms. "Yes!"

"I know you have plans to meet with your sister and Jade. But baby could you take a rain check this time. I have plans for us? I wish I could have told you sooner, but I couldn't because I wanted our engagement to be a surprise. We're going on vacation."

"No need to explain honey. Of course, I will let them know I have to reschedule. I'm sure they would understand. Besides I could use a vacation."

"I love you Charlie."

"I love you back."

Malcolm and I finally made it back to Chicago after a seven-day getaway in Las Vegas. I've enjoyed the unlimited shopping sprees, fine dining, penthouse suites, the casinos, more importantly the love of my life, my husband Malcolm.

The ladies and I met up as soon as I touched down.

"Look at you, looking all happy," Chloe teased.

"Well, marrying the love of my life and getting to spend time with him in Las Vegas will do that to you," I gushed.

Jade and Chloe rolled their eyes.

"Anyway, are you ready to do this? I'm so excited for ladies' night out. You know the Jamaican Jerk Villa is everything," Chloe said as we pulled up in front of the building.

"Drinks are on me," I said.

Jade wrinkled up her nose, "You mean on Malcolm. You better watch yourself. You're a married woman now. He won't like other guys hanging out with his woman."

"Who said anything about other guys? I have the only man in the world I want. He's got nothing to worry about," I said as I noticed someone walking toward us.

"Hey, ladies. Drinks on me? What are you having?" Paul asked.

Chloe and I exchanged glances.

I nodded. "Go ahead."

"I think we want Mai Tais," she said.

As I scooted into my seat, my phone vibrated. I knew who it was – Malcolm. I figured he'd be worried.

The first text said: Is everything okay?

I responded with, "We're good. Paul is here too. He's going to buy us drinks. Isn't that nice? Anyway, you don't have to check up on me. Paul will take care of us.

It took less than two seconds before he called me, we were in the middle of giving our drink orders.

I whispered into the phone, "Hold on a second." I ordered a Mai Tai Martini. Before I could get back on the phone, I saw him walk in. "Malcolm? What are you doing here?" I asked.

He walked over and grabbed my hand, pulling me to him.

All the color in Paul's face drained out.

"Guess what?" Chloe asked. "I'm pregnant."

Paul looked like he wanted to faint. He didn't say a word as he turned and walked out.

Poor Chloe looked mortified. She ran after him.

"Wait," I said, but Malcolm motioned for me to let them go.

A few minutes later, she returned alone, saying that Paul got an important text and had to leave.

Malcolm asked, "You know what? This isn't the kind of place you want to celebrate in. I know a better place. Let's go."

We walked outside and the first thing we saw were the flashing lights. Police were everywhere. In the middle of the street, a bullet-ridden car took center stage. It was Paul's.

"Paul!" Chloe yelled.

A police officer stopped her. "Who are you?"

"I'm his girlfriend," she said as she tried to get past the officer.

"He's been shot. He's on the way to the hospital," the officer explained.

My breath caught in my throat. How did this happen? Why?

"We have to get to the hospital. Can you drive us?" Chloe asked Malcolm.

Out of all nights, this would be the night it seems like we're getting stopped by every traffic light. A black car pulled on the side of us. The passengers rolled down their windows pointing their guns. It's a hit, I yelled. Malcolm pressed the gas and drove as fast as he could. Chloe and I scream as bullets fly throughout the car.

"I've been hit." Chloe cried out loud.

"Chloe's been shot Malcolm." I screamed.

We lost the driver of the other car which is a sign of relief. My life flashed before my eyes. So much has been happening these past months. It's like when you think things just couldn't get any worst, they did. I love Malcolm, he is my husband, and I know that I vowed for better or worse. But the bodies around us are dropping dead left and right.

I hold the towel against Chloe's arm to slow down the bleeding. At least until we arrived at the hospital. "How's she doing?" Malcolm asked.

"I could be better." Chloe replied in agony. "You know something Malcolm. I'm starting to get this feeling that your bad news." Chloe added. To be honest I have the same feeling. The only difference is, she's telling him to his face, while I'm holding it in. The look of hurt is clearly all over Malcolm's face. There is no one I can agree with my sister now. He would be devastated. The last thing I want him to feel in this very moment is that I'm against him when I'm all the family he has left.

Besides this is what comes with this lifestyle. "Malcolm is not bad news, Chloe. How dare you say that about my husband."

"You're right. I'm sorry. It's just everywhere we go, something bad happens."

"True. However, it isn't Malcolm's fault."

"I'm sorry you feel this way. I will never put you or Charlie in harms way. Malcolm added.

"I've been shot twice while in your presence." Chloe replied.

"We know. We were all shot at. It's some things going on that I can't discuss right now.

"He's right let's just focus on getting you to the hospital. I added." Chloe started yelling and kicking the back seat. I try to calm her down.

Malcom

"Mercy Hospital is only a few minutes away. Calm down. It's going to be okay," I said to calm Charlie and Chloe as I sped down the street.

Charlie hadn't stopped shaking since we'd jumped in the car. "Slow down, please. Just slow down. We don't need to get into an accident." I could tell she was trying to be the strong one. Chloe was panicking. That was to be expected. She had the baby to think about. My feelings about Paul didn't matter. What was important was that baby in her belly.

We pulled up at the emergency room. I ran around the car, signaling for a valet to run. "She's been shot. She's pregnant. We need to get her inside."

He jumped into action, calling for security to help him. He told the officer, "We have another gunshot victim. She's pregnant."

A medical team ran outside to meet us. They quickly placed Chloe onto a gurney and began assessing her wounds and asking questions. I had to stop Charlie because all her emotions had finally caught up to her.

I stopped a nurse and said, "It's a flesh wound. I think it just grazed her."

She looked at me as if I was some sort of criminal. She didn't know me. She had no right to give me that look.

The staff took her back to triage for several minutes before sending her out to the waiting room.

"What happened? Why did they send you back out here? What about your arm?" Charlie asked.

Chloe shook her head. "I'm good. We need to worry about Paul. He's in surgery. The nurse is going to find out how it's going for me."

"What about the baby?" Charlie asked. "Shouldn't they be concerned about you?"

I couldn't focus on them now. From what I could see, Chloe was fine. She was up, talking, the nurses decided her injuries weren't bad enough to warrant putting her in a room yet. She was good. I had something more important to worry about. If I didn't move now, I didn't know if I'd ever get the chance.

A nurse came out and said, "I can take you up to the waiting room upstairs if you want to wait for news about your boyfriend."

Chloe didn't need to be asked twice. She grabbed Charlie's arm and said, "Let's go."

They started to walk away, then Charlie noticed I wasn't following them. "What's wrong?" she asked. "Don't you want to go upstairs with us?"

"Hey, I'll be back," I said.

"Where are you going?" she asked.

I took a deep breath, wanting to take a minute to clear my head. "I have to take care of something. I'll be back soon. I promise."

She didn't protest, but I could see the worry in her face. I think I'd already let her see too much. She wasn't dumb. She knew how dangerous the life could be. I hated myself for getting her involved. It wasn't her fight to fight, but at the same time, I couldn't imagine life without her by my side. I just needed to get through this time, then, she and I could live a normal life. No more drama.

By the time I arrived at North Avenue Beach, my whole crew was there, just as I requested. I scanned their faces as I took a head count. I needed them to be ready to go because things were going to go down today. One was missing.

"Where's JC?" I asked.

No one knew and that was a problem. They knew to keep tabs on each other in case anything happened.

I gave directions while we waited for him to show up. When he did, my blood boiled over. Who did he think he was? I'm not some chump he can disrespect.

I held my hand out before he could get a word out of his mouth. "Give me your phone."

He gulped. "Huh?"

"Your phone!"

His hands trembled as he handed it to me. What did he have to hide?

I scrolled through his text messages while he laughed nervously.

Too bad there's nothing to laugh at.

I aimed my 9MM at him to prove this wasn't a joke.

"What are you doing?" he asked.

I looked at my crew. "Looks like our boy made a move on his own. That move put us all at risk. Innocent lives could've been lost tonight."

JC's teeth began to chatter. He knew what was coming next. If he didn't, he'd soon find out.

"He ordered a hit on Paul. That guy is fighting for his life right now," I explained.

JC said, "Wait. Let me explain. I heard Paul was behind the death of your mom and brother. I handled it for you. We can't let him get away with that. If you'd stepped up to the plate and handled your business, you'd know that he's not the guy you think he is. I was looking out for you." He shoved me.

Boogie and Tan exchanged knowing looks. Boogie rubbed his hands together like he knew something. I knew what he meant, but his suspicions didn't always ring true.

I still hadn't taken my gun off JC. He pleaded with me, "We've known each other since what? Third grade?" He tried to push the gun out of his way and make a move on me, but I wasn't having it. I held too much anger in my heart and someone needed to pay for it. It had to be him.

I pistol whipped him until he was nothing more than a mass of blood.

"Put him in the trunk," I ordered.

As Boogie and Tan followed my orders, my mind went blank. No rage. No anger. No tears. Just a blank, hollow well that no one and nothing could ever fill and make whole again. My family was dead. The two people whom I loved the most in the world were gone. That shooting might as well have taken my life too. I was dead inside. Now others would have to die too.

One decision. One move against someone I'd considered my friend for almost all of my life made me bitter and ashamed. I used to be a proud guy. Proud of my basketball talents. Proud of my life choices. Proud of my family. I lived with pride. I was set to have it all. Today, I stand here feeling anything but pride. I feel shame. What happened to JC, what I made happen to JC didn't give me any sense of pride. It made me feel more miserable than I'd already felt.

"What do you need me to do?" Keon asked.

I glanced at the trunk of my car. Inside was my friend, bloodied because of me, because of an order I'd made, because anger fueled everything I do these days.

"Take him to the Museum Campus at the 11th Street Station," I ordered.

"Please, please, please," JC begged for his life.

I didn't say a word as I plunged the machete into his throat and watched his severed head rolled to the other side of the trunk. Rage took over as I dismembered him. With each slice I felt a visceral pain run through my veins. First, his fingers, then, his throat. Then, his head. Methodical. Sadistic. Maniacal. That's what I'd become. A monster. A menace to society. A dark shadow in a sea of darkness. This was personal. Tragic and sad, but deeply personal. He was my friend. I never imagined that my life or his would ever come to this, but this is where we ended up. Tragedy built upon tragedy. Hurt on top of hurt.

Tan, Boogie, and Keon stood stalk still, looks of horror in their eyes. Hardened men by any standards were now afraid of me. I know they wondered if my sudden turn on one of our own was a prelude to what was to come for them. Honestly, I wondered the same thing. Who knew how all this would play out in the end? If it meant mass destruction and more deaths, I would handle it. I had to. I had no other choice.

"Get him out of here. Spread his body parts all over the railroad tracks. Don't make it pretty. Don't make it easy for someone to identify him. Don't do the cops' job for them. I want to send a message to you and to anyone else who thinks I am someone who will live my life in fear," I said.

Now I hold all the power. I am respected. I earned it with true grit and more muscle than I ever thought I had. From now on people will be with me or they'll be against me. The choice is theirs. If they cross me or choose to work against me, they will be killed on site. No questions asked. There won't be time to beg or plead. It won't help them or their cause. I no longer care about others' feelings. I don't care how their loss will damage their families. The person who tore my world apart obviously didn't care about me or my feelings. They took my family and rode away like nothing happened, like the people inside our vehicle didn't matter to anyone. They were wrong.

Everyone needs to know I'm no one to mess with. Everyone will fear me and that's okay. I want it to be that way. I need it to be that way. It will make my mission easier.

"We need to get the word out to the neighborhoods," I announce.

"What word? Which neighborhoods?" Boogie asked.

I slow down to make sure he doesn't miss a word. No sense in having to erase another friend right now. I'm sure they'll be plenty of time for that later. Eventually, everyone will get their due.

"Theo needs to know I'm coming for his corners," I said.

Tan blinked a couple of times. "You are? Which corners? He's got a lot of spots all over the city. Southside, West Side, up north, everywhere. Which spots do you want?"

I cocked an eyebrow at him. "All of them."

He gulped.

"Riverdale, Fuller Park, South Deering, and Washington Park. I want them all," I said.

"Do you think he'll just give up his corners like that? I mean, he's not going to walk away without a little push back. Are you prepared for that?" Tan asked.

I nodded. He was right. "I don't think he'll give up his corners that easily either, but I'm not worried about that right now. We'll handle that when the time comes. If he wants to get out of pocket, I'll buy and send his mother a black dress."

Keon added his thoughts, "We might be able to get him to pay us a cut of his profits. That might be a better route to pursue. It makes sense. It could be like a win-win."

I shook my head. "Nah, I'll win both ways. We cut a deal. Let him think he's gotten over on his, then, we kill him." I walked away before they tried to talk me out of it. I was done talking. No more negotiating. No more taking people at their word. No more letting people walk all over me. No one wants to feel my wrath. Not now. Not ever.

After my meeting, I had work to do. I had evidence to get rid of, things to destroy, traces of my actions had to disappear for good. I went to one of my secret homes and cleaned the filth of the day's events off me. I needed the time to clear my head and put my mask back on – the mask that I let Charlie see. She knew me like that. As much as it pained me to pretend to still be that guy, I did it... for her.

An hour later I arrived back at the hospital.

"You're back? What took you so long? I missed you," Charlie said as I lifted her into my arms.

"How's Paul doing?" I asked.

She shrugged. "He's okay I guess. The doctor's said he's in stable condition."

"Have you seen him?" I asked.

She nodded. "Yes, but he's been asleep for hours. He still hasn't said anything to us. I don't think he knows we're here."

I nodded.

"Do you want to see him?" she asked.

I shook my head. That wasn't a good idea. Not now. I had stuff I needed to work out in my head. If the stuff JC told me was true, then, I had another problem I had to deal with. Seeing him would only muddy the waters. I needed time to clear my head. Charlie needed me now, so she'd be my priority for the rest of the night... I hoped.

"No, we can come back to see him tomorrow. Let him get his rest. He probably needs it," I said. "We all do."

Charlie hugged Chloe goodbye. "See you later, okay?"

Chloe nodded. "Yeah, but could you do me a favor and swing by my place and get me some clothes?"

Charlie scanned her bloodstained outfit. "Yeah, sure. We can do that for her, can't we, Malcolm?"

"Sure. No problem." I didn't want to refuse her. How would that look? I gave Chloe a hug. "Don't worry about it. We got you covered."

She breathed a sigh of relief, looking down at her outfit. "I hope I never see these clothes again." She looked around the room. "I hope I never see any of this ever again."

The next morning, I was awakened by the smell of bacon.

"Did you sleep well?" Charlie asked when I pulled the covers over my eyes.

I peeked out from under the blankets. "I don't know yet. Ask me in an hour."

She yanked the pillow out from under my head. "Wake up, sleepy head. It's a new day. Let's go check on my sister and Paul."

I reluctantly rolled out of bed and dragged myself into the shower. "Give me fifteen minutes."

By the time I came out, Charlie had breakfast ready for me.

"Aw, thanks. I'm starving." I said. "You know what? I think we should skip stopping by your sister's place."

"What? Why? She needs new clothes. She can't stay in the same clothes another day," she protested. "We can't do her that way."

I hadn't explained myself well, so I started over again, "No. I mean, let's stop by the Water Tower Place and get her some brand-new things."

She pursed her lips.

"Seriously," I said.

"Let me get this straight. You're offering to buy Chloe new clothes? What? Now you're shopping for her? When did that start happening?"

For a second, I thought she was being serious, then, she started laughing.

"Relax. I'm just messing with you," she said. "So, the Water Tower Place? Fancy."

I forgot how new all of this was for her. "It's on the way. We can stop and buy her some clothes and whatever necessities you think she needs. I think that's better than digging through her house."

MALCOM

"Good morning. We come bearing gifts," Charlie gushed as she hoisted over-stuffed bags full of everything any young woman her age could ever want and more. After the second armful of stuff, I stopped paying attention to what Charlie picked out for her. Whatever she felt she needed was cool with me.

"Is all of that for me? Dang. Someone likes to spend all their money," Chloe said as she stood to take the bags and pull out all the items. "So, you do love me, brother-in-law?"

"All right. All right. I did my good deed for the day," I said. "How are things?"

She glanced over her shoulder at Paul. "He was awake, but the doctor's said it's better if he rests. It will help him heal better. They've been keeping him sedated with medication. He's in a lot of pain." She teared up as she spoke. "Thank you for... for everything. I mean you were there when it happened. You helped us survive. You got us out of there. You were here with us at the time and you're here now. Plus, look at all these fancy clothes you got me. How can I ever possibly thank you for everything?"

"That's what family is for. You are my family," I said. My phone interrupted our conversation. "Hold up. I'll be right back. I have to take this."

"That was quick," Charlie said when I walked back in the room a few seconds after stepping out.

"Are you okay here for a while? I have to take care of something," I said.

No one protested. I think they'd gotten used to me having to take care of this or that all the time. It's the way things operated these days for me.

"Okay, but is there anything wrong?" Charlie asked.

I didn't want to tell them. It would only add to their stress.

She eyed me a you better talk now look. "What happened?"

"Okay. Promise me you won't panic. I'll handle it."

She crossed her arms in front of her body. "That depends on what it is, Malcolm."

There was no way to sugar coat it. "Boogie has been shot and killed."

"Oh, my God. I'll go with you," she said.

I shook my head. "No. You stay here with Chloe."

I turned and nearly ran into Big Ace, Paul's #1 hitman.

Charlie sensed trouble. She grabbed her Celine bag with one hand and Chloe's hand with the other. "Hey, you know what? I forgot to tell you. I need you to help me decorate. You love decorating. Come on. It will help get your mind of stuff here. He can rest. I'll bring you back later." She grabbed my arm on the way out. "Who is the other guy?"

I hadn't focused on him yet. "That's RIP."

RIP and Big Ace nodded their hellos and sat down while they waited for us to leave.

I was adamant about Chloe not knowing where we lived, even in this situation. But that's about to change. "I'll be back soon," I said as I walked away and phoned my realtor about a property I had my eye on in Winnetka. "Yeah, you know that place we talked about? Well, I want to make an all cash offer if we can close immediately."

I felt a sense of relief as I hung up the phone. The chaos would be over soon enough, then, I could reveal the place to Charlie and we could go on with our lives, but first, I must figure out what to do about Chloe. If she's with Paul, she can't be in our lives. Before I say anything to Charlie about my suspicions, I needed confirmation.

CHARLIE

"It smells like you're cooking your famous French toast," Chloe said as she flipped through channels on the 85-inch television screen that hung over the wood-burning fireplace. "Are you almost done? My stomach is growling like crazy."

I flipped the chocolate chip pancake I'd made especially for her. She used to love flavored pancakes when we were kids. My mother used to make an elaborate breakfast every Sunday morning after church. "Hold on. I'm finishing up the pancakes. Girl, I went all out for you. You better not be lying about how hungry you are." I poked my head out the kitchen pass-through. "Pancakes, eggs, home fries, bacon, sausage links and patties, and – you're going to love this – freshly squeezed orange juice. Does that sound like a lot of food? Wait. Don't answer that. The answer is yes. I pulled out all the stops for you. Do you know why? Because I love you."

She clapped her hands and giggled. "Ah, you just admitted you loved me. That's so sweet." She stopped talking as breaking news came on television. "Charlie, get in here. The sheriff is holding a press conference."

I turned off the stove and ran over to the television to see if it was news about the attack on us. "Turn it up," I said as I took the seat next to my sister.

The sheriff stood with a grim look on his face as he waited for the reporters to settle into place and a team of uniformed officers took their places behind him. By the look on the other officer's faces, something very serious had happened.

"Ooh, it must be something big," Chloe said.

I shushed her. "Just listen."

The sheriff stepped up to the microphone and went through the formalities of introducing himself, spelling his name for reporters, and laying the ground rules for the press conference. He said, "Please, hold your questions until after I've given you all the information I have in front of me. I'll try to answer as many questions as I can, but understand, the situation is still very fluid, and some things simply can't be disclosed yet. At least not until we've completed our investigation."

Cameras were clicking and flashing all around him. He squinted at the bright lights and began his statement.

"A short time ago," he glanced back at an officer over his left shoulder before he continued, "at just after eight this morning, a discovery was made on the railroad tracks near—"

A reporter interrupted him, "Which set of tracks? Do you have the location?"

He rolled his eyes. "Like I said, I can only disclose some information. It's a very fluid situation – meaning we're actively investigating what happened and how this could have happened."

Another reporter asked a question, but he shut it down before more questions flew at him. "No, listen, I'm trying to tell you what I can." He took a step back, seeming to wrestle with whether or not to proceed. Finally, he returned to the microphone. "This morning, savvy civilians found a disturbing scene while out for a walk. Human limbs were found scattered over railroad tracks on the near northside. That's all the information I can give you about the location. There was a severed head and both upper and lower limbs."

There was an audible gasp in the room.

He looked directly at a center camera and said, "We will find the person responsible for this heinous crime. Whomever he or she is will be located. We ask that you – citizens of our community – be mindful of your surroundings. If you see something, say something. If you have any information about what may have happened here, please, contact police. You can remain anonymous. Someone knows something. Nothing happens in the vacuum. Thank you." He walked away from the microphone as reporters shouted questions at him.

We hadn't heard Malcolm walk in the room. His eyes were fixed on the television. "What was that?"

Chloe shrugged, "They found some body parts by the railroad tracks. They don't know who did it. They're asking the public to come forward with information."

He gulped.

"It's crazy, right?" I asked. I walked over to him and hugged him. "I'm making breakfast. I hope you're hungry."

He tore his eyes from the screen and hugged me back. "I'm starving. Let's eat."

I shook my head. "Not yet. Give me five minutes to get it all served up, then, we can eat."

He kissed the top of my head. "Will do."

When he walked away, I asked Chloe, "Can you help me take the food to the dining room?"

She jumped up and helped by gathering large platters and dishware while we discussed what we'd just heard. I nibbled on a slice of bacon as I fixed a plate for Malcomb, then, all of a sudden, I started to feel nauseous. I shoved the plate in Chloe's direction and ran down the hallway.

When I returned, she asked, "Are you okay? What was that?"

The nausea still hadn't subsided. I held my stomach. "I don't know. I think I must be getting sick. I haven't been able to hold down food lately."

Chloe cocked an eyebrow at me. "Uh oh. You know what that means, don't you?"

I scoffed at what she was trying to imply. "No way. It's just a bug."

Malcolm returned to the room. "I hope you're not talking about a bug in the food," he teased as he took his seat. "Wow! This is amazing. Sit down. Let's eat."

I picked at my food to make it look like I was eating it, but I couldn't bring myself to eat. The sight of the food made my stomach churn. My head hadn't stopped spinning. The smell was nauseating.

With a mouthful of food, Chloe said, "You don't look so good."

I closed my eyes for a second. "I'm okay."

Malcolm stopped mid-bite and asked, "Is everything okay?"

I didn't have time to answer. I had to get out of there. I ran to the bathroom again.

A few minutes later, I walked back into the dining room and tried to act like everything was perfectly fine, but in my head, I knew it wasn't. I was no dummy. I knew what my symptoms could mean. I just wasn't sure I was ready to admit them to Malcolm and Chloe or to myself. I needed to know for sure.

"Are you sick? Do you need a doctor?" Malcolm had a heart of gold when it came to me. He always worried about me.

"I'm okay," I lied. "It's probably just the flu." I hated to lie to him, but with all the stress he'd been under lately, he didn't need me to add anything else to it. At least not until I know for sure.

He gave me that look. It was the one that told me he knew I was trying to hide something.

"What?" I couldn't hide my joy. I knew what the symptoms were trying to tell me.

He stopped eating and walked over to me. As he wrapped his arms around me, he whispered, "Is my baby having my baby?"

Before I could admit or deny it, my nosy sister jumped out of her seat, spilling her glass of orange juice all over the place. "You're pregnant! I knew it! I knew it!" She pointed at my belly. "I told you. I knew it."

I didn't know if she was happy with excitement or angry. It was hard to tell. "Wow. We're pregnant at the same time. How did that happen?"

Malcolm quirked an eyebrow at her. "You don't know?"

She chuckled. "You're so bad. Stop that." She sat down, a look of concern on her face. "Let me help clean this up, then, I have to go to the hospital to see my other baby. Do you think you could give me a ride?"

Malcolm nodded. "Yup. Let us know when you're ready. I have to go celebrate with my babies."

She made a sour face. "I don't want to know. Go do what you have to do but keep me out of it."

He laughed.

She realized what she'd said and bury her head in her hands. "You're so wrong."

We arrived at the hospital two hours later.

"How's my man?" Chloe walked into Paul's room and pulled back the curtain.

"Excuse you?" a pregnant woman was standing at Paul's bedside, her hand in his.

Chloe stopped dead in her tracks.

"Who are you?" I asked.

Chloe found her voice. She looked at Paul, venom in her eyes. "Really? Really? You think you can do me like this? To our child?"

The woman grabbed her arm and turned her around. "Baby?" She scowled at Paul. "Did you tell your little pregnant girlfriend about your pregnant wife?"

Chloe didn't focus on Paul's wife. Her anger was with Paul. He did this to her.

"You think you can play me? You think I'm that girl?" She clicked her tongue. "I'm not. You're not going to do me like this."

The wife giggled. "Let me help you. Obviously, you're clueless about who this man you think you love is." She waked over to Paul and smoothed her hand over his muscular arm in a possessive manner, as if she was toying with Chloe's emotions. "Your baby doesn't matter. No one cares. If Paul made you feel special, I can assure you, he didn't mean any of it. He never does."

Chloe's lip trembled.

Paul tried to intervene. "Kay don't do this right here."

"Kay?" Chloe asked.

"That's my name, sweetheart. Kay. You've never heard him mention me before?" She smiled a sinister smile. "I'm not surprised but let me let you in on the best part of Paul's story. Your child will be baby number six for him. Many women have been fooled by him before you. I'm sure there will be more. Paul's on a mission to make sure he spreads his virus as far and wide as possible. You might want to go get yourself tested. My husband has HIV."

Chloe collapsed to her knees.

I pulled her to her feet to get her out of there before Kay gave her anymore devastating news. "Let's go."

Chloe was like a ragdoll in my arms. She went limp.

"It's going to be okay. I've got you," I said. As I walked her outside, I told her about Malcolm's parents. I'd never disclosed that information to anyone before. "We'll take you to a clinic to get tested. No matter what happens, I'll always be on your side. You hear me? I got you."

"Negative," Chloe said when she walked out of the clinic. "I think Kay was trying to scare me away. I'm sure the story about all the other babies was a lie too."

"Let it go. That was two weeks ago. It's over. You can stay with me and Malcolm as long as you need to. Don't worry about a thing," I said as we climbed into the car.

"I'm hungry. Can we go through a drive-thru?" Chloe asked.

"Nope," I said. "We're going to eat a good dinner at Alinea's. We could use some cheering up, don't you think?"

Chloe took my hand and squeezed it. "Thank you for everything. Things can only get better from here."

We drove in silence.

When we reached the restaurant, the driver stopped in front and opened the door for us. We got a table right away. Fifteen minutes after our meal arrived, Chloe kept checking her phone.

"What are you looking for?" I asked.

She sighed. "I haven't been able to get ahold of Paul. He's not answering my messages."

I didn't want to yell at her, especially in front of a restaurant in front of people. I looked around the room. That's when I saw him. Chloe noticed him at the same time.

"Please, don't tell me that's who I think it is," she said as she pushed her seat back.

"Don't," I urged her. It was too late.

She marched to his table and confronted him and the unsuspecting curl with long, loose curls and ruby red lips.

I couldn't hear her words, but I heard the splash of her drink when it hit his face and dripped down to the floor.

Malcom

I drove at slow speed as I searched for Mooch. He'd done a good job of hiding from me, but I was onto him now. I was in his neighborhood. His time was up. A person can run, but they always have to resurface, and today, I had no doubt he'd come out of hiding. People like him always do when they think they've gotten away with something. If my mother and brother's murder had taught me anything, it was to never forget.

Mooch murdered my friend. Now he has to die.

"There it is," I said, almost salivating at the sight of his mother's house. "If you won't come to me and make this easy, I'll come to you and kill his entire blood line."

It was simple enough. A slow crawl down the 3500 block of W. Wilcox wouldn't cause alarm. I wasn't blasting music. I was alone in an expensive ride. I wasn't a threat on the surface. In fact, in some neighborhoods, I'd be a mark. I'd be the one all the thugs would want to keep an eye on as they waited to make a move and snatch it from me.

The house came into view like a beacon of light on a dark, dreary night. That's what it felt like when I let my emotions dictate how I lived my life. I became a different person. I turned into someone I despised, but I needed that hate-filled person to survive.

I pointed the Glock toward the house and fired.

Screams erupted through the thick night air. That's what I wanted. They got the message. Give me Mooch or pay the repercussions.

By the time I made it back to my crew, I assumed Mooch had crawled out of his hiding place and had come looking for the person who'd shot up his momma's house. I reloaded my gun, checked the AR-15, and walked over to check up on my crew.

Keon and a few others were hanging out, minding their own business, not all phased by the gunfire I'm sure they'd heard. It happened so often in the hood, it had become like white noise to our ears. No one flinched unless the guns were aimed at us.

I knew every car in the neighborhood. We all knew who belonged and who didn't. One of the cars didn't belong here, but I kept my cool and kept my eye on that car as soon as it started to move.

My senses were heightened as it pulled out into the street and slowly crawled up the block.

A hand extended out the window. My gut told me to get out of there, but when that hand waved, I squashed the feeling in the pit of my stomach. I thought I was being paranoid. That was no way to operate. I had power. I had control. I had my guns nearby if anything went down.

The car picked up speed and passed by us. I couldn't make out who was in it, but when they passed without incident, I breathed a sigh of relief. I'd live to see another day. That's all that mattered.

I fell back into a conversation with my crew.

"You know that car?" I asked.

Keon glanced in the direction of the car. "Yeah, I think so. I've seen it around. They're cool."

I nodded as I watched the car go around the corner.

When it came back around the block, every cell in my body told me to move. No one came around a second time unless they had some business to take care of.

I yelled, "Get down!"

It might have only been a couple of seconds, but it felt like hours before my crew realized what the problem was. It was too late. The noses of several Glocks and AR-15's was pointed at us. The pop, pop, pop deafened me as the shooters fired in our direction. One guy went down almost instantly. Two more fell in quick succession. Dead. I'd seen that look on someone's face before. I knew what death looked and smelled like. These guys – not yet thirty years old – were dead. Their lives were cut short because of me.

Keon fell next, holding his arm as blood gushed out of it like a sieve. Despite his own suffering, he yelled, "Stay down, Malcolm. Don't let them get you."

It struck me like a knife. He'd just been shot, the others were lying in pools of their own blood, and all he cared about was me. He wanted to help keep me alive. What had I become? Why was my life suddenly more important than his?

The next two weeks were filled with non-stop funerals. Mothers crying. Baby mamas clung to closed caskets. Flowers and thoughts and prayers were all anyone could offer, yet, they fell short of what those who were suffering really needed. I'd been in those devastating shoes. No amount of prayer, praise to God, or flowers would bring back the one we lost. We were living in a war zone. It was inevitable more deaths would come. Someone always had to pay for what someone on their crew did. That was the code. I lived by that code. I'd contributed to that ideology.

Preachers espoused the sanctity of life and the healing that comes from celebrating those we lost. Newscasters climbed and crawled every surface to get images of the aftermath of street justice. What we did to each other, in our neighborhoods, won them accolades. They may not have known it, but their incessant coverage of the mounting death toll only made things worse. It gave us information that might not have made it through the hood yet. They added fuel to the fire in the streets. They had no idea what was going on behind the scenes.

As the body count rose, talks began between both sides of this ugly game. Mooch agreed to have his crew stand down. I pushed for a truce... for now. This was only the beginning of what was to happen. A truce would ease the tensions and make them think they were safe, then, when I thought they'd had enough, I'd come back for more.

CHARLIE

"I have something to tell you," Chloe said, sounding tentative. "But before I do, I need you to promise me that you won't get upset."

I gave her the side eye. "What is it now?"

Any time she was nervous, she'd stammer and get this wide-eyed look on her face like she had now. "I did something, but don't worry, I know what I'm doing."

"What did you do this time?" I asked.

She rang her hands together. "Wait. Let me explain first. I didn't know it would happen."

My stomach clenched. "What is it? You're making me nervous."

She squeezed her hands tightly together. "He called me."

"Who called you?" I wanted to scream.

She stopped, took a deep breath, and blurted, "Paul called me. He wanted to meet with me, so I did it. Just once. I thought if he wanted to apologize, I could let him. No harm in that, right?”

I couldn't believe her. “Have you lost your mind?”

She gulped.

“Chloe?” I couldn't be mad at her. I recognized the look on her face. She was a girl in love. Even if it was the wrong guy, I could never hate her for it.

“He wants to work things out.”

I held my tongue while she tried to convince me how sincere he was, but I knew what this was. He didn't want to work things out because he suddenly had an epiphany. This was about something else. I didn't know what exactly, but I was for sure going to keep my eye on him. I didn't trust him or anything he had to say.

“I don't trust him,” I said. “And you shouldn't either. I get why you wanted to speak to him, but that doesn't mean you have to believe anything that comes out of his mouth.”

She shrugged. “He was under a lot of stress. Haven't you ever done anything you regret? I know I have.”

“He'll hurt you again, Chloe,” my voice broke as I spoke. “I can't stand here and watch that happen. I love you and you know I'll support you in anything you want to do, if it's right, but this isn't it. This doesn't feel right.”

“What do you mean it doesn't feel right? Maybe not for you, but that's because you never liked him. He was never good enough for you. He's not Malcolm. He can't be perfect, but he's perfect for me and my child. I know it,” she protested.

“He's using you. You're a pawn in some sick, twisted game. If he cared about you, he wouldn't have lied to you and treated you like trash,” I said.

The look on her face broke my heart. My words hurt her.

"Why can't you ever just be happy for me? Why are you the only one who deserves love? I'm somebody too." She stormed out of the room.

I wanted to chase her and make her see what she'd gotten herself into, but our emotions were too raw. We needed time and room between us to work out our feelings, then, we could talk.

I sat down on the sofa and waited until my nerves settled. I couldn't erase the thought that if I didn't stop her, I'd lose her. That was my biggest fear. When I thought enough time had passed, I walked to her room and leaned on the door, whispering, "I'm sorry, Chloe. You know I'm just looking out for you. I can't stand the thought of him hurting you again. I don't want to see that happen."

Chloe opened the door, tears pouring out of her eyes. "I can't do this with you right now. Please, leave." She shut the door in my face.

"Oh, you're talking to me now?" I hadn't heard Chloe say a word in days.

"How's the saying go? They always come back?" Chloe teased.

I held my tongue, so I wouldn't ruin whatever was about to happen.

She cleared her throat before continuing, "I don't want to say you're right, but I get the feeling Paul isn't being honest with me. I don't want you to tell me how dumb I am. I just want to talk."

This had gone on for far too long. She had to know. "Sit down."

She blinked twice. "Why?"

"It's time you know." I waited for her to sit down. "I hired a private investigator." I stopped her before she had time to argue with me about it. "I only did it to help you. I told you, I didn't want to see him hurt you again. The private investigator has been following him for the past few days."

She gulped. "I can't believe you did that. What did they find out?"

It broke my heart to have to do this to her. I almost didn't want to go on. "Paul is still very much married. That woman at the hospital is still his wife. He has no plans to divorce her. Before you say anything, there's more. Proof." I left her there while I went to retrieve some documents the private investigator had given me. When I returned, Chloe had shored up her strength and was ready to confront me.

With her hands on her hips, she stood in the doorway. "There you go again, Charlie. You just put your nose where it doesn't belong. As long as it doesn't touch you or your precious man, it's all good, then, right? You know what you can do with your secret files and your sneaky private detective? You can stop. Just stop! Look, here's the bottom line, I'm tired of living here with you and Malcolm anyway. I want my own place. I want a family too. A real family. I want to be happy. Is that so hard to understand? I've been running wild doing this and that and don't have anything to show for it. I don't have anything of my own." She brushed tears from her cheeks. "You have Malcolm. He's a great guy. He's always done for you. Why can't I for once have someone like that in my life?"

I shed my own tears for her. How heartbreaking to hear her say those words!

She continued, "You have a husband and several fancy places to live. That's not to mention the unlimited shopping sprees, the fine dining, and everything else. Your life is perfect. You're about to have your first child. You're glowing and happy." Her voice caught in her throat as she spoke. "I can't do this anymore. I can't be here with you. Not like this. I deserve a life too and if you can't get with that, then, I can't be here. I'm moving in with Paul." She turned to find Malcolm in the doorway.

"What? You're leaving?" Malcolm asked. He looked at me, but I didn't know what to say. I was too stunned by her announcement. I thought my research would have changed her mind. "You can stay here as long as you need, you know? You can even move into one of our other properties if you want some privacy. I don't have a problem with that. So much has happened. I feel like it's my job to protect you and Charlie. I want what's best for everyone, but if you want to leave with Paul, I guess, we support you. Always. No matter what."

His words sounded so heartfelt, but I had the feeling they pained him to say. He loved Chloe like family. He wanted what was best for her. I just hoped Paul wouldn't do something to ruin his view of her.

The next morning, Chloe was all packed up and ready to go.

"I guess, that's it," Chloe said as Malcomb placed the last box in the truck. "Hug?"

Malcolm hugged her first.

I waited. Saying goodbye to my sister, even though I knew she'd be close, made me sad.

"You can't hug your sister? You're too good for me now?" she teased as she pulled me in for a hug. I wanted to cry, but I forced away the tears. They wouldn't help.

I said my goodbyes and watched as the vehicle moved away into the distance.

Malcolm grabbed my hand. "She'll be fine."

I shook my head. "I don't know. I just think Paul is up to something. I feel like he's just using her as a pawn."

Malcolm hugged me harder and kissed the top of my head. "I don't think that's the case. I think those might be the hormones talking."

"Stop that." I laughed. "You know what I mean. My gut tells me something is wrong."

"Not going to happen." He took my hand and led me away.

I told myself it'd be okay. Malcolm was no fool. He promised to protect us. I had to believe him.

"Ready to go to your first lesson?" he asked.

"We're really doing this?" I asked.

He nodded. "You need to learn to shoot. Hopefully, you'll never be in a position to have to shoot, but I think we'll both feel better if you at least know how to protect yourself."

"You're right. I will, but that doesn't mean I'll like it."

I couldn't help but giggle as he rubbed my belly. "If you don't stop, I might turn into Buddha."

He laughed. "Good. I'll have my own personal Buddha belly. I love it."

After the shooting range, we'd stopped to pick up some ice cream and sandwiches from a Cuban place around the corner. Even though I was sad to see my sister go, I had to admit, it did feel good to have Malcolm all to myself. We needed that time. It wouldn't be long until the baby arrived and our whole lives would change again.

Malcolm started to speak, then, the lights went out.

"See what you did," I teased. "I told you to stop rubbing my belly."

When it didn't come back on, he jumped out of bed and ran to the window. "They still have power across the street."

I shrugged. "It's probably a fuse."

He ducked back away from the window. "There's a car with no lights on coming up the road. Get down!"

I froze.

He jumped for me and slid me off the bed. "Get in the closet." He pulled my gun out of the nightstand drawer and pushed me toward the closet as he ran out of the room.

He and I have never experienced anything like this while at home. "No one knows where we live Malcolm, I don't know why you are acting paranoid." I said.

"Right now isn't the time for this. Do what I ask."

"I was just saying."

I heard you. But Charlie you have to trust me on this one. Do what I asked. I'm going downstairs to make sure that all is good."

"I want to come with you. Don't leave me up here alone. I'm scared."

"It will be quick."

"Ok. Hurry up."

My heart is beating very fast. I feel as though I'm living my life in a horror movie. I thought as Malcolm left the bedroom.

Malcom

I ran with my senses on high alert. First, I bolted through the kitchen, into the family room, then, I saw them. Two shadows, dressed in black, wearing masks. I didn't hesitate to pull the trigger. Two shots. One man falls down dead. The other, injured and begging me not to kill him, collapses to the ground next to his partner.

I walk over, telling myself not to kill him, and pulled the masks off their faces.

"RIP?" I had to laugh. Of course, it's Paul's muscle and Kilo Paul's brother. Who else would be involved? Who else wants to hurt me and my family? I didn't have to ask him anything. I knew why they were there. I knew who sent him. I pulled his cell phone out of his pocket and dialed Paul's number.

"Is it done?" he answered.

"No." One word is all I needed to get my message across to him, but I had to dig in and make sure he'd spend the next few hours of his life in fear. "I'm coming for you."

I pointed the gun at Kilo as he begged for his life. He shouldn't have come for mine is all I could think. With Paul still on the line, I pulled the trigger and shot him dead before I disconnected the line.

Another shot rang out from upstairs. I bolted toward the stairs as sirens blared in the distance. I had to get to Charlie.

She was trembling in the doorway, terror written all over her face.

"Come on," I said as I grabbed her hand. "We have to get out of here."

She retreated. "No. We can't run. If we do that, they'll investigate us. Do you want them to find out about the life we live? We can just tell them that they broke in. It was a home invasion. We did what we had to do to protect ourselves."

Blood pooled by her feet.

"Is he dead?" she asked, pointing to the man she'd shot.

I nodded and guided her away from the door. "We have to work fast." I grabbed all the cell phones from the men and tucked them away just as the police arrived at the front door.

"They tried to break into the house," Charlie said so convincingly, I believed her.

An officer looked around the room. "Looks like a home invasion gone bad. This happens all the time. You'd think these guys would know better than to mess with someone's home. Just so you know, they had a lookout driver. The guy tried to take off, but we caught him. He's dead."

I leaned against the wall. All the pieces were falling into place. We'd get away with it.

Another officer stepped inside. His eyes went wide when he saw me. "Hey, I know you. Aren't you that basketball star? Man, if I had your talent, I'd jump at every opportunity I could get. I never had any real skills. I never got the chance to go to college. Have you decided what school you'll go to next year?"

"No. I can't think about that now. We have a baby on the way." I grabbed Charlie's hand. "How long are you going to be here? It's been a long day.

The officer promised they'd be out of our way very soon.

After the dust settled and the police were long gone, it was my first opportunity to reassure Charlie.

"I've made a big decision," I started. Charlie glanced up at me with weary eyes. "I'll contact a realtor in the morning and put the house on the market. Obviously, this isn't our happy home anymore. We can start over, somewhere else."

Charlie didn't react.

"Did you hear what I said? What do you think?" I asked.

She nodded. "I heard you. I'm just distracted. I've been trying to get in contact with Chloe, but I haven't been able to get ahold of her. I guess all this craziness has stirred up my emotions. She hasn't answered my calls."

"She will," I assured her.

Charlie sighed and wrapped her arms around me. "I know. I'm just being paranoid."

It took us a long time to settle. Charlie drifted in and out of sleep in the guestroom while I cleared up the mess and tried to rid our lives of the most recent devastation. I was too wired up to sleep myself. One thing had to happen before I would ever relax again.

When I went to check on Charlie for the hundredth time since she'd laid down, her phone rang. I breathed a sigh of relief, believing it was Chloe calling, but when I picked it up to take it to her, it was a number I didn't recognize.

"Charlie, your phone is ringing," I said as I tried to wake her.

She grabbed it before her eyes were completely open. "Chloe?" Her shoulders slumped as the caller responded. "This is me. What's wrong?" She put the phone on speaker.

Chloe begged, "I need your help. I had to get out of there." She fought to get the words out in between tears. "I overheard Paul talking about the hit he sent on you and Malcolm tonight. He said he was the person responsible for killing Malcolm's brother and his mother. She was an accident, he said. He didn't know she would be in the car too. She was in the wrong place in the wrong time." Her voice shook. "I want you to know I didn't give him your address. He used my car earlier and must have gotten your address from the navigation. That's the only way he could've gotten it. I swear, I didn't give it to him."

Chloe's heart sank. "Where are you?"

"I'm at the BP on W. Van Buren."

Malcolm said, "We're on our way. Stay out of sight."

Charlie warned, "Get rid of your phone. You don't know if he's tracking it."

She whimpered, "Okay, but please, hurry. I'm scared."

I raced down the street, taking lights, cutting corners, broke ever driving law possible to get there. My gut told me she wasn't okay. I didn't have any inside knowledge about her or anything that went down between her and Paul, but I knew how these things worked. Someone always had to pay the price for perceived or implied wrongs. I just hoped my hunch was wrong.

Charlie vacillated between anger and terror. Nothing I said or did soothed her. Her panic increased my anxiety. I hated that there wasn't anything I could do to calm her nerves.

"We're here. I'll go in first." I jumped out of the car and ran toward the front entrance, but true to form, Charlie was hot on my heels.

A gunshot has a distinct sound. Once you hear one, you never forget. Somewhere in the back of your brain, the sound lingers, waiting like an animal ready to pounce on its prey. It haunts you when you close your eyes. It's there, lying in wait.

"Was that a gunshot?" Charlie asked in response to the pop, pop, pop.

"No, no, no." I sped up.

When we reached the threshold, Charlie's hands shook as she reached for the knob. "Chloe!"

I covered her hand with mine and turned the knob. There she was. Lying on the floor, blood pooling under her head, undressed from the waist down.

The blood-curdling scream that Charlie emitted was like nothing I'd ever heard before. Filled with an unmistakable anguish, her cries rocked me to my core. It was both primal and almost religious in nature. "No! No! Why?"

It took several seconds before I could gather my thoughts. I'd failed them. There was no doubt in my mind that this was all my fault.

Charlie had the presence of mind to want to preserve Chloe's dignity – at least what was left of it. In one fell swoop, she pulled her jacket off and knelt in front of her sister to cover her exposed skin, tears dripping like a waterfall from her face. I couldn't take my eyes off her, off the disaster that was in front of me, then, the pops started again.

"Get down," I ordered as I shrouded her with my body, using my back as a protective shield. Out of the corner of my eye, I noticed the car – dark colored – roll past, passenger side window open.

As if I had stepped out of my own body and watched the scene from afar, I saw myself pull my gun out of my waistband and fire at the car. One. Two. Three. The front window shattered on impact. A shrill scream reverberated through the night sky. The car careened off the road and slammed into the building.

"Stay here," I ordered before running out the door to catch the shooter before he got away. Within a few seconds, I was out the door, on the sidewalk, standing outside the driver's side door and firing shots at the driver. I didn't know who he was or where he'd come from, but there was no doubt in my mind who'd sent him. Three. Four shots are all it took.

Satisfied that he'd never see the light of day again, I secured my weapon and turned on my heels to get out of there before someone saw me, but then, I saw Charlie. She lay on the ground, bleeding and unresponsive.

"No!" I screamed. My hands shaking, I pulled out my phone and dialed 9-1-1. "No! Charlie, stay with me. I'm right here, baby. Stay with me." Everything happened so fast. I don't know how long it took for the police and paramedics to arrive. The wait nearly killed me, but thankfully, we made it to the hospital before it was too late.

"She's pregnant," I announced as they unloaded the gurney from the ambulance. "Be careful with her. She's pregnant."

Someone escorted me to a waiting room while doctors worked on Charlie. I don't recall what I said or if I said much more than to take care of her and our baby. The next thing I know, a doctor is standing in front of me, a grim expression on his face.

"What is it? Is she okay?" my voice shook as I spoke. My whole life flashed before my eyes.

He nodded. "She and the baby are fine. Thankfully, the bullets missed her vital organs and bypassed the baby altogether."

I jumped up, elated. "Can I take her home?"

He shook his head. "I'm afraid not. I'd like to keep her overnight for observation."

"You said she was okay. Why do you want to keep her?" My heart dropped to the pit of my stomach. What wasn't he telling me?

"She is okay, but after all that's happened, I want to be extra cautious," he explained.

"Where is she? Can I see her?" I didn't wait for a response. It didn't matter. No one was going to keep me away from her. I barged in through the emergency room doors and yelled, "Charlie?"

A group of nurses jumped.

One pointed to a door on the far end of a long corridor. "She's in there. Are you family?"

"Yes," I said as I made a beeline for her room. I had to see her. I had to find out for myself if she was okay.

"Malcolm?" She blinked back tears.

I stared at the wires snaking over her like a coil of snakes. An oxygen line, a heart monitor, a fetal heartrate monitor, a blood pressure cuff. "I'm so sorry." Tears spilled from my eyes. "I don't know what to say."

She started to cry. "Chloe's gone."

I grabbed her, but she winced as I touched her. "I'm so sorry, baby."

My phone buzzed in my pocket.

She scrubbed tears from her eyes, but that didn't prevent them from flowing freely. "Why? Why did this happen?"

My phone buzzed again.

She took a deep breath. "You better answer that."

I felt like a horrible human being for leaving her, but I had to take the call. "What up, Keon?" I answered. "What is it? I'm at the hospital."

He blurted, "I got eyes on Paul. How's your girl?"

I refused to answer questions about Charlie. She was mine. No one needed to know anything. "Where is he?"

He gave me all the details. I told him how to handle it and returned to Charlie's bedside.

"What happened?" she asked as she fought to keep her eyes open.

I ran my hand down her cheek. "Go to sleep, baby. I'll be right here." The faster I could get her to sleep, the quicker I could leave to take care of Paul for good.

Oak Park was only minutes from the hospital, but in my rush to get this over with, the drive felt like long, agonizing hours. I'd memorized the address and arrived without any problems. It was even easier to get inside the home undetected.

Luckily, he was in the shower, oblivious to my invasion. I reached for the doorknob just as a cell phone rang.

Paul stopped the shower and answered immediately. I could make out what the woman on the other end of the line said, but I heard his every word.

"I'm out of town on business," Paul lied to the woman.

Paul pulled a pocket door on the other side of the bathroom open and sauntered to the bed to continue with his call. As he settled in, he leaned over and pulled a gun out of a pair of pants lying on the end of the bed. He sat on the edge of the bed and said, "I see you've found me. I told you I was coming for you." He snickered. "Look, I'm sorry, man. I didn't mean for any of this to happen."

I didn't have time for this. I wanted him dead, but at the same time, I wanted to watch him suffer for everything he'd done. "Yeah, sure. That's why I'm going to kill you slowly. As a matter of fact, I think I'll get creative and give your demise a theme." I pointed my weapon at his big mouth.

"Drop your weapon right now," a man shouted from behind me as he shoved the nose of a gun in my back.

I had no other choice. I did as he said.

"Stephanie," the man yelled.

A woman emerged from the bathroom.

The man turned his anger on her. "Who are these guys?"

She gulped, her hands trembling, "I can explain, Dalvin."

The man held a hand up. "No. Don't. Why is there a naked man in our bed?"

Things just got interesting. I'd found a way out. All I had to do is make it believable.

I raised my hands. "I have no business here. This is a personal matter. I don't know your wife, man. I'm not here for her. My business is with him." I pointed to Paul.

The man assessed the situation, then, shook his head. "I'm a cop. I could kill all of you and get away with it."

"No need for that. Let me take care of that for you. You see the naked dude? He knows why I'm here. We have history. Ugly history. I don't want to get into it, but—"

The cop interrupted me, "Let me guess. You came all the way here to kill him?"

I didn't know how to respond.

"Here, take this." He handed me his gun. "I want you to kill him. You won't go down for this. You have my word."

I took the gun and pointed it at Paul.

"Go ahead. Why don't you get it over with already? I'm dying as it is. You can kill me now or wait for AIDS to finish the job," Paul said.

"What is he talking about, Stephanie?" Dalvin asked.

She whimpered.

"First, you cheat on me in our home and now this?" He placed his head in his hands. "I came home to surprise you." He pulled a lottery ticket out of his front pocket. "We won." He laughed. "Well, I won. twenty three million dollars. Yeah, I won. How could you do this to me?" He pulled something out of a dresser drawer. "Take these."

He handed four pills to Stephanie. "They're Ambien. Go ahead. You like them, don't you?"

"No, baby, please," she begged.

He pointed his gun at her.

She cried as she swallowed the pills.

"You," he said as he pointed at Paul. "Put the pillow on her face and don't move it until I say so."

It took her only seconds to die as Paul held the pillow over her head.

"Now, you can finish. Go ahead. You want to bang my wife, why don't you do it one more time for old time's sake."

I backed out of the room. "I don't think I should be here for this."

The cop yelled, "No, you'll stay here."

My stomach churned as I stared at the wall. I couldn't watch. After a few horrifying minutes, he yanked Paul off his wife and told me to kill him.

Despite what I'd just witnessed, I wanted Paul dead. "You destroyed everyone's lives. You killed my brother, my mother, my sister in law Chloe, and you almost killed my wife Charlie and my baby." Without thinking twice, I cocked the Glock 9. I wanted to do this slowly, but you're right, I should get this over with." I fired one shot.

Dalvin pointed his weapon at Paul's chest and fired several rounds. "Leave. Now!"

I made it back to the hospital. Charlie was still asleep when I made it back to the hospital. I was glad. I needed the time to clear my head. I flipped through channels on the television and stopped on Fox 32 for breaking news. The story was about a cop, who had returned home from work to find his wife dead following a violent sexual assault. He shot and killed the suspect.

"He kept his word," I whispered as the realization hit me. It was over.

Hours passed before Charlie finally stirred awake. I leaned over her and planted kisses on her lips as tears sprung from her eyes. I held her as tightly as I could without hurting her.

"We'll get through this together, I promise. Right now, for the sake of the baby, you need to relax as much as possible. I know you're in tremendous pain. I know I've put you through so much, but we need to think about our child. Chloe would want us to have a healthy baby. All I'm asking is that you try not to think about what happened last night. Push those memories out of your mind. Chloe is still with you. She'll always be with you. She'll see our child grow. I promise you, we will lay her to rest right and mourn her properly when all this is over. We'll remember all the good times. When the baby is here, we'll share her memory. We'll tell her story, but for now, we need to concentrate on getting our child here. Do that for me?"

She nodded as tears continued to flow down her cheeks.

Malcom

"What a year!" I said as I sat on the floor next to Charlie and our baby MJ.

Charlie kissed me. "It sure has, but let's not talk about the bad stuff, okay? Let's just enjoy this beautiful baby."

The doorbell rang. No matter how much time has gone by, I still couldn't embrace the idea of inviting someone into our lives. Keeping my family safe was the most important thing in my life.

"I'll be right back," I said as I made my way to the door. "Officer Dalvin?" I didn't know whether to slam the door shut in his face or to punch him for showing up out of nowhere.

"I quit my job. I'm not a cop anymore," he said. "I have enough money to spend the rest of my life on the beach if wanted to." He seemed nervous. "I stopped by to check on you and your family. How is everyone?"

"Fine."

He smiled. "I never thought I'd say this, but I've been getting counseling to learn how to deal with my illness in a positive way. Part of that is to learn to be thankful for what I have. To do that, I want to thank you by giving you this." He handed me a check.

"Two million dollars?" I couldn't believe my eyes.

"Yes, use it to clean up your life. Get away from here. Take your family, your young son, and live right. The whole reason I joined the police force was because I had a dad who was into dirty deeds. He lived by the street code. They ruled his life. He was dealing and stealing and doing all kinds of stuff. It was a fast life. The streets took it when I was five. You don't want that for your child. That's no way to live."

I called Charlie over. "Bring the baby." I made the introductions.

She seemed so pleased to see it wasn't some thug from the street, she told him he was welcome anytime.

I showed her the check. Her breath caught in her throat. "Is this for real?"

Officer Dalvin said, "It sure is. I want you to do good. Be a family. Love and take care of each other. This money will help you do that."

I took my little boy in my arms and introduced him. "This is Officer Dalvin. He's a good man. He's family now. Don't ever forget that."

That money did get put to good use. It put me through Real Estate school. I opened my own brokerage firm and went legit. At least that what Charlie thinks. Charlie opened a store in memory of her sister, selling personalized gifts to honor lost loved ones. Baby MJ is growing fast and getting cuter every day. He's smart, strong, confident, and most of all, being raised in a safe, loving home with parents who will do anything for him.

I called Charlie and informed her that I will be working late tonight. The truth is I'm handling business.

Where are we headed?" Keon asked as I passed by all the usual spots.

"We have a meeting," I responded. "It's probably better if you don't ask any questions when we get there. I want to see what's up with this guy first. I need to see if he's legit or just fishing for information about what I have going on."

Keon gave an obligatory nod and turned his attention to the radio, fiddling with buttons.

I gave him the side-eye. "Are you done? Anything else you want to mess with in my car?"

He shrugged. "Nah. Sorry. Didn't know the radio was off limits."

Another side-eye and he figured it out.

The address was a little difficult to find. I thought I knew every square inch of the city, but apparently, I was wrong. Moss had a spot I didn't know about yet.

"Can you at least tell me why he wants to meet?" he asked, referring to Moss, my connect's underboss.

I pulled in front of a nondescript Chicago turn of the century of a three-story walk-up. "I think this is it. Keep your eye out. I'm going to pull into the alley to scope out the back. I don't want to walk into an ambush."

"You think your connect would set you up?" Keon asked.

I shrugged. "I think anything is possible," I said as I scanned the block. It didn't look any different from any block on the southside of Chicago. People were out and about, huddled together for meaningless conversation. Anything outside was always better, even if the city boasted more threats than they'd seen in decades.

After a quick check of the block, I squeezed the car into a space down the block and made my way to the house with Keon right behind me, looking out for anything that moved.

"Are we good?" I asked as we reached the wrought-iron gate.

"Yeah, we're good. I got you," he said, his head on a swivel for anything that looked unordinary. "A curtain moved up on the third floor. Is that where we're going?"

I nodded. "Let's see what this dude wants."

We didn't have to ring the buzzer for him. As soon as we stepped inside the vestibule, the sound of heavy boots hitting the wood stairs filled our ears.

"This is it," Keon said, reaching for his gun.

I waved off his concerns. "Keep it cool. Nothing has happened yet."

He pulled his shirt over his waistband and held back. "He's alone?"

Moss was dressed in head to toe Gucci wear, looking like a man who liked to flaunt money he didn't have. Everything in our business was connected to something else. There were rules to this game. Some of us put our money into things that mattered, like our cars, our ladies, and our other legitimate ventures. Moss was the kind of guy who liked everyone and their mama to know he had something. That's the first sign of someone who grew up with nothing and got into the game too young.

"Come on up," Moss said as he waved us in.

Keon stepped in front of me, his hand precariously close to his weapon as he followed Moss up the winding stairs. When we reached the door, he asked, "Do you want me to wait out here for you or come inside with you?"

I glanced inside the door. On the surface, it looked like any other person's house, but who knew what would go on behind closed doors. "Come inside and watch the door for me."

Moss snickered. "You don't have to do that. This is a conversation between brothers."

His words were like a gut punch. "We're not brothers. I had a brother. He's gone now." Saying the words, brought back all the pain, but I squelched it. That was something I had to learn to survive these days. I couldn't carry that pain on my shoulders all the time.

Moss sat at the head of a long dining room table and motioned for me to sit opposite him. "I have a proposition for you."

I nodded.

He slid a bag across the table to me. "Tell me what you think of this. I figure, you're doing well for yourself now. Too well. You might want to think about diversifying your inventory."

I didn't have to look at it too long to know what it was, and it wasn't premium.

I stood up. "You trying to play me?"

He stood, his hands in front of him in a defensive posture. "Nah. Nah. What do you mean?"

Without another word, I kicked my chair back and motioned for Keon to move, so we could bounce.

"What was that?" Keon asked.

I shook my head. "We gotta make another stop before this fool paws that off on someone else."

"What stuff?" Keon asked.

We only had to drive about ten minutes before we arrived at my connect's place.

"What's up? You have a pickup to make?" Keon asked.

I was tired of listening to his nonstop questions, I had half a mind to punch him in the mouth, but I'd promised myself and Charlie that the drama would be limited. We'd had our fill.

"You're like a toddler. Do you ever shut your mouth?" I asked finally.

He stopped, jaw slackened. "Yeah. I'm not a toddler."

I didn't have time to watch him mend his wounds. I had to let Gerald know about his guy.

"Malcomb," he said when his security let me through the door. "What's up? Did I miss an appointment?"

I shook my head. "Nope, but you missed Moss."

His eyebrows quirked up. "Moss? Where did you see him?"

"His house," I said.

Gerald leaned forward, his meaty elbows sliding across the table as he sat down at his desk. "Why were you at his house?"

"He called me," I said.

"And?"

"And he tried to sell me some counterfeit heroin," I said.

Keon coughed. "What? Is that what he did?"

I shot a glare at him. "Yeah, that's what he did."

Gerald leaned back in his seat and pulled out a cigar and lit it. "Impossible. We don't do fake."

I studied his demeanor. It wasn't right. He wasn't outraged like he should've been. Fake product always comes back to bite the dealers. He should've been worried.

"Did you hear what I said? It's bogus product," I tried again.

He blew a smoke chain over his head, then, locked eyes with me. "I'm going to tell you something."

I leaned forward. "Go ahead."

"My friend Moss is playing dirty. I suspected he was behind some missing items lately, but I gave him a pass because we're family. I try to treat my people right, but if what you say is true, he'll ruin my business and take food from my family's mouth. I can't let that happen," Gerald said.

One of his security guys walked over and whispered something in his ear.

Gerald took another toke of his cigar. "Looks like Moss isn't just dealing bad product. He may have had something to do with what happened to one of my men Liam. According to word on the street, he's turned state's evidence, which means it's time for him to go. Why don't you give him a call and tell him you changed your mind about the transaction?"

I didn't hesitate. This was business after all. Better him than me.

In less than 15 minutes, Moss was there, eager to earn what was coming to him.

Gerald waved him in, called him over, and busted a cap on him. He slumped to the floor in one fell-swoop. Dead. Gerald's crew watched in stunned silence before following orders to remove his sorry carcass.

The next morning I gotten up and showered as if nothing happened. I didn't want to let Charlie know or show her any signs of me being back into the streets dealing again. She would be devastated. She threatened to leave me if I returned to my past life. I don't want to lose my wife or my son. They're all I have. She could never find out about this.

"That was more beautiful than I imagined," Charlie said as she laid the baby down for a rest after a long day at the church for the christening.

I nodded as I watched her move with such ease. I couldn't believe my luck. I had the perfect family – the one I'd always dreamed of, here with me.

After she got the baby settled, she said, "I'll be right back. I left my purse in the car."

I winked. "Don't be gone long."

She narrowed her eyes at me. "What?"

I loved when she got riled up. I offered a pout. "I'll miss you."

A quick roll of her eyes and she was off, mumbling something about how silly she thought I was.

I remained in the baby's room, listening to the sounds of my sleeping child. Who knew a baby could change your life so much? Ten years ago, I would've never imagined how much I'd love to have a child. I thought my life was going to be basketball and all the perks that come with playing ball. Now, with a family, I couldn't imagine leaving them to play basketball. They were my life. My everything.

A jarring sound caught my attention. I moved out into the hallway and peered out toward the door. It sounded like a scuffle.

"Charlie?" I was already on the move toward the door.

As I got closer, there was no mistaking what the noise was. I instinctively reached for my gun and with a quick glance over my shoulder to make sure the baby was fine, I used my shoulder to shove the door open.

It took a few seconds for reality to hit me. First, a shot, then, Charlie collapsed to the ground in slow motion, with blood oozing from her head.

I fired without thinking, wanting to kill whoever did this. A man falls to the ground while another gunman barreled through me and heads to a white van with a carpet cleaning company logo spread across the side.

I fired again as the van sped off. I was torn between helping Charlie and wanting to kill the people who did this. As one man lay dying and Charlie's small body lies prone on the cold, hard ground, my life, everything I'd worked so hard for fell apart. I crumbled to the ground next to her and held her in my arms as tears streamed down my face.

"Wake up, baby. Wake up," I said, not realizing how violently my body was shaking.

Charlie gurgled as she tried to speak. Tremors caused her to shake. I removed my coat and wrapped it around her to keep her warm.

"Please, baby. Please." I looked at the dead man and screamed. "Why?"

When I looked back at Charlie, blood gushed out of her mouth. Her lips trembled as she fought for air.

"Help! Help me!" I don't know where the words came from. They didn't sound like mine, but, yet, I knew the desperate cries came from me. In a matter of seconds, I went from a man who had it all to a broken man.

One final gasp, blood trickling from her mouth, a pool of blood soaking through the coat, and Charlie was gone. Dead. In my arms.

MALCOM

They say there's a numbness that comes with the death of a loved one. I say that's true, but there's also a deep, horrible anger that eats at your soul. As I sit here, in this church, the same church Charlie and I christened our child in, I can't help but want revenge. I know what I want to do. I even know what I'll do. The question is when? Tomorrow, I'll bury the woman I love. Tomorrow will be the last time I'll ever see Charlie's face. Tomorrow must be the day her killer dies.

"How are you holding up?" Keon nudged me out of my thoughts as he took the seat next to me.

"I'm not," I mumbled.

Conversations had been tough to get through. It's funny. People don't know how to act around you when someone you love dies. They mean well. They try to say the right thing, but the truth is nothing they say will ever be right. Nothing will ever erase the pain. The hugs, tears, promises to be there for you, and the flowers don't ease the heartache. I've been down that road too many times before. I know none of it works, but, yet, I accept their condolences and pretend they'll do me some good. Nothing will until the coward is lying in a pool of his own blood, wishing he could get another day with his family.

"What do you need? Name it and I'll do it," he said.

I checked the room to make sure we were alone. "I know who killed Charlie."

Keon sat up straighter. "Who? How?"

I leaned back in my seat. "I had this dream about her."

He gave me that look – the kind that said he sympathized with me.

"For real. I saw her in a dream. She wrote the guy's name in blood," I explained.

He bit his lip and gave me a slow nod as if to placate me.

"She told me who did it," I raised my voice.

He nodded again and whispered, "I believe you. Who was it?"

I looked around again and said, "Not here. Just know that the person responsible for her death will pay for what he did. His whole family will pay for this. His entire bloodline will feel it. The whole city of Chicago is about to mourn. They won't get away with this."

I arrive home after celebrating the life of Charlie.

I wrapped my arms around my Aunt Mona. "Thank you for doing this."

She squeezed me back. "You don't have to thank me. We're family. Moving in here to help you with that precious baby isn't a sacrifice. It's a reward. You need me, and quite honestly, I need the two of you." She kissed my cheek before planting her gaze on Lena, her longtime friend and overly flirtatious wannabe cougar. "As for her, don't go there."

I lifted my right hand in the air. "Don't worry about me. I'm not having any of that. I'm not even thinking about that. Charlie," I said as my voice broke like it often did when I spoke about her, "Is my heart. She always will be."

Lena licked her lips as she assessed me up and down.

"See. Who does she think she is?" Aunt Mona's finger was wagging as she approached her to give her a piece of her mind.

I had to laugh because the idea that my aunt thought she had to speak for me was the most normal part of my life lately.

After a long day of going through the motions and trying to keep my emotions in check, I finally fell into a fitful sleep. Lately, my dreams were filled with visions of what happened that day. I couldn't stop thinking about it.

I heard her voice, but like the countless other times I'd heard her voice since she passed, I waited for the sound to leave my head. I couldn't allow myself to fall into that abyss. She was gone. I was alone with our child and nothing I ever said or did would bring her back.

"Malcolm." This time the foot of the bed shifted as if someone sat on the edge.

As much as I tried to ignore, tell myself that it wasn't real, my heart told me to look. It was just one look. A sign. A confirmation that it was all in my head. When I opened my eyes, there she was in a white robe with white, fluffy angel wings on her back.

I jumped up, knocking my foot into the nightstand in the process. "Charlie?"

She offered the same sweet smile I'd learned to love so many years earlier. "Malcolm."

I fell to my knees, tears spilled from my eyes. I could see and hear her.

A bright glow framed her body.

"Charlie? Is it really you?" I could barely get the words out of my mouth. "How?"

She shook her head. "I'm so sorry. I never wanted to leave you."

Through my tears, I forced the words I'd wanted to say, "I love you, baby. I love you so much. I'm sorry I didn't protect. I'm sorry for letting you down. I'm so sorry." All the pain, rage, and anguish I'd felt gushed out of me like a dam had broken. My whole world was right there, and I couldn't do anything to make her stay. This was my punishment for all the wrong I'd done, all the wrong I'd brought into our lives. "It should have been me. Why didn't God take me? Take me!" I fell forward and reached for her hand, but it slipped through. I couldn't feel her touch. I couldn't hold her in my arms again. She was here but not here with me in this world.

She whispered, "You have to be strong. Our child needs you." Her voice started to fade. "I'll always love you, Malcolm. That will never change. You are my heart. Please, be strong."

"Don't go," I begged as the light faded. "No, baby, please don't go. I need you. I'm a mess without you. We need you." I don't know how long I laid there, but when I finally came up for air, my face was covered in tears. She was gone. Again.

Now it's time for me to get Eternal Revenge on the cowards that killed my wife. I can't stop. I know it's wrong, but it must be done. I can't go another day knowing the people responsible for destroying the most important part of my life are still out there, living, breathing, pretending like they've done nothing wrong. They will die.

That's what I tell myself as the body count rises in the city. Anyone who played a part, associated with, knew, loved, laughed with Gerald and his crew must die. All of them. I don't care where they are, what they're doing, or who knows about it, they must die.

As they lay lifeless, I'll move up the food chain and find Gerald. He was supposed to be my guy, my friend, my partner. How could he do this to me? To Charlie? What had she ever done wrong? In my heart, I know her only sin was sticking by me. In a weird way, her death is my fault. I brought this life upon us. Now I must make it right.

"You found me." Gerald said. He had the nerve to applaud as I stepped in the door. He acted like this was one big game and I was his pawn. Had I let him intentionally think that? Had I played right into the palms of his hands?

"You're not as dumb as I thought you were," he mused as he finished clapping at my expense. "You actually put this together. Tell me, did you do it by yourself or did you need help from a friend?" He snickered. "Oh, that's right. You wife – what was her name again? She's dead. Too bad."

I wanted to kill him with my bare hands, but for the first time in my life, I froze as he continued to insult me and the woman I loved.

"You know why she had to die, don't you?" He didn't wait for a response. "Now you know what it feels like to lose someone you love. It's awful. It makes you want to hurt people. You go out and hunt for victims because the pain in your heart is too great. I'm afraid that's what happened in this little situation."

"It's not a little situation. She was my wife, the mother of my child," my voice broke as the harsh reality hit me in the face. He'd had her killed, but for what reason?

"Do you know the names of the people you've had killed? Did you even bother to ask what their names were?"

I didn't respond.

"One of them was my son. You killed my child. My flesh and blood."

I swallowed hard. Who was his son? I looked around the room, searching for clues.

"Right there. Look at his face," he ordered.

On the shelf next to Gerald's desk was a picture of him and Jack, a man I'd killed a year ago.

"You killed my son," he said it a nonchalant manner, as if it was just another day in the life, but the hatred in his eyes was unmistakable. He wanted me dead, but what he didn't know was how badly I wanted him dead. So badly, I could feel the heat of anger rising in me like an inferno. This was war.

Gerald wasn't done inflicting pain. "So, in case you haven't figured this part out yet, your brother," he paused to laugh, "that was me. I orchestrated that. Your mom, though, she got in the way. Oh, well."

I held my hand on my gun. "Why?"

He shrugged. "Your brother should've known better than to touch stuff that doesn't belong to him. Didn't your pretty mother ever teach you that?" His gaze fell on my gun. He moved to grab his gun out of a desk drawer, but I was ready for him and jumped to block his arm before he touched it.

Kojo, Gerald's bodyguard, was in the room in less than a second, his gun at my head. "I wouldn't do that if I were you, Malcolm."

These people were fools. Did they think I didn't do my homework before I walked in the door? I sneered at him.

"How can you defend a man who got your wife pregnant?" I asked.

"What?" Kojo's hold on his weapon loosened. "What are you talking about? How do you know my wife is pregnant?"

I came prepared. I pulled a stack of pictures out of my back pocket. "I have a PI on my team. What do you have? Nothing more than a boss who bedded your wife. Look for yourself."

Kojo snatched the pictures out of my hand.

Gerald pleaded with him, "That's not true. I can explain. It's not what you think it is."

I had him there too. "But what about these text messages? I pulled a folded-up phone report from my pocket. "We got your text messages. There it is, in black and white."

Kojo fell against the doorjamb, his gun cocked as he read the text messages Gerald exchanged with his wife. He pointed the gun at Gerald.

"You hiring, Malcolm? I'm done here," he asked.

There was no need to respond. Our response was the firing of our weapons until our clips were empty and Gerald was little more than a heap of bloody trash on the floor.

As we walked out, I called Keon on my cellphone and said, "I've got a mess for you to clean up. Bring the good mop and make sure you take out the trash."

It's been very hard living without Charlie. I miss her so much even though she still visits MJ and I. Keon and I are officially out of the game. We have a lot of real estate in which we either sell or lease. We started a record label, putting money behind local talent to help their dreams of becoming an artist come true. I don't want to cause anymore hurt to my city. Those days for me are over. At least for now they are.

www.ingramcontent.com/pod-product-compliance
Lightning Source LLC
Chambersburg PA
CBHW031254060726
47590CB00003B/897